ESCAPE & EVADE

JT SAWYER

OTHER TITLES BY JT SAWYER

THANK YOU

Thank you for buying this book! I hope you enjoy reading it as much as I enjoyed researching and writing it.

Join my email list at JTSawyer.com if you would like to receive notifications on future releases or the FREE copy of *Lethal Conduct,* a short story within the *Search and Destroy Series*.

PROLOGUE

WEST AFRICA

FIVE YEARS Earlier

THE SERENITY of birdsong in the jungle canopy was disrupted in a micro-second as an RPG hissed across the emerald valley floor. From his concealed position in the treeline, Nathan Hendrix had fixed his sights on the first of four cargo trucks meandering along the overgrown road nestled along the rugged borderlands between Sierra Leone, Guinea and Liberia.

The missile struck the union between the engine and the driver's compartment, incinerating the two mercenaries inside and causing the truck to careen slightly before coming to a halt.

A second later, one of the fighters on Hendrix's left discharged his RPG, sending another messenger of destruction into the rear truck, obliterating the front half and sealing in the two vehicles in the middle.

Hendrix grabbed his AK-74 and began dumping the potent 5.45 rounds into the mercenaries exiting the remaining vehicles while the rest of his six-man team did the same with their rifles. The hasty shooting match lasted less than thirty seconds, filling the muggy air around Hendrix with the acrid smell of spent gunpowder.

When it was over, he scanned the road in either direction then raised his hand, giving the signal for five of the men to accompany him towards the convoy while one fighter remained behind to provide overwatch.

Though there were no outward indicators, Hendrix knew, without reservation, that these trucks belonged to the Rohrbach Mining Corporation out of Johannesburg, whose mercenary-led army had been ravaging the West African countryside during the past few months of civil war. The brutal raids upon the mining communities had become a familiar pattern in this remote valley that rarely saw outside aid or made international headlines.

But the same group responsible for decimating the native villages would now be providing the funds to allow the native Gola fighters with Hendrix to start new lives in Guinea, away from their ancestral lands in northern Liberia.

Hendrix moved slowly across the open field. The streaks of charcoal camouflage on his tan face had blended with his sweat, causing a rivulet of black veins that made him resemble some primeval creature. His tattered clothing and mud-encrusted boots were as worn out as he was from years of jungle living.

The sticky humidity caused the thick smoke emanating from the two mangled trucks to linger like an ominous black cloud over the valley as Hendrix and his men flowed through the knee-high grass and onto the road.

Approaching the splayed bodies on the ground, he and his men swept their rifles along the dead, ensuring there wouldn't be any surprises.

While two of his men stood guard at either end of the road, Hendrix and the others searched the contents of the cargo trucks. Most of the vehicles contained looted goods: water barrels, food crates, medical supplies, excavation tools and boxes of personal belongings pillaged from the dead.

But the second truck in the convoy held the coveted payload, stolen from the mine foreman's safe house. A cast-iron strong-box the size of a mini-fridge was strapped to the rear of the bed. Hendrix could see from the parallel lines scored into the metal bedding of the vehicle that it had been dragged into place with cables.

He removed his backpack, retrieving a ruggedized box, then pulled out a small clump of Semtex, attaching the blasting charge to the safe's door beside the lock. When it was secure, he inserted the tip of a timing device into the Semtex, setting the digital clock for thirty seconds.

Upon depressing the timer's red button, he scurried out the back, waving for his men to move towards the rear of the convoy. The resulting explosion was barely enough to startle the monkeys in the nearby treetops.

He waited a few seconds for the cloud of dust and debris from the tailgate to disperse then returned to the bed of the truck. Climbing inside, he plucked through the safe's contents until he found what they'd come for.

The riches he discovered in the safe not only had the potential to greatly improve the lives of his own men but, to his utter surprise at discovering one small leather pouch in particular, could one day profoundly alter the fate of an entire nation.

CHAPTER 1

BLAYNE, Utah

THIRTY-TWO MILES NORTHWEST of Four Corners

NICK MERCER STOOD on the rear tire of his Ford F-150, doing a final pass with the polishing cloth over the juniper-slab table in the bed of the truck, pausing on occasion to inspect the polyurethane coating for any scuff marks.

It had taken him only a week to finish the custom kitchen table for a client in Moab, and he always relished letting his eyes linger on the finished product as the morning rays of sunlight teased out the fine grain.

He had obtained the juniper from his Navajo friend, Eddie Peshlakai, whom he cut firewood for in the fall west of Halchita, Arizona on the reservation, southwest of his home in Blayne. This particular piece contained long natural streaks that imparted a unique pattern to the wood and that had saved it from Eddie's woodpile.

The original two-foot-wide slab had come from the base of an immense old juniper and had become four feet through Nick's careful cutting, gluing and joining of the book-matched pieces. Now, after shaping, sanding and finishing, the transformation would yield him eight hundred dollars and potentially more work from the new client.

He stepped down, walking around to the open tailgate and inspecting the angled wrought-iron legs that were screwed firmly into the underside of the wrist-thick wood then stood up, flinging the polishing rag down on a nearby folding chair beside his toolshed.

"Well, what do you think...should we drive her up to her new home?" he said, glancing over at a black-and-tan cattle dog lounging on the front porch of his small cabin.

Luce briefly lifted her head, yawning, then leaned back against the railing. Though he'd originally named her Lucy after rescuing her as a seven-week-old pup on the Rez, he felt Luce was a better fit but hadn't bothered to correct the difference on her tarnished nametag. The three-year-old dog didn't seem to mind either way.

Mercer placed several cotton blankets on the juniper tabletop then a thick layer of bubble wrap, finally securing the entire thing with a latticework of old tie-straps and manila rope.

When he was confident the load wouldn't shift, he went back into his cabin and finished his coffee then grabbed a green daypack, his brimmed hat and a banana. When he headed back out to the porch, Luce was already waiting by the driver's side of the truck.

He let the screen door slam behind him, not bothering to lock the place. Mercer had bought the old cabin four years ago, shortly after moving to the area, drawn to the isolated location in a region that boasted over eleven million acres of high-desert wilderness, most of which was accessible out his back door.

The cabin was built in the 1940s using ponderosa pines harvested in the Blue Mountains to the north. The nine-hundred-square-foot abode was perfect for his needs but, most importantly, it was secluded.

There were only two other neighbors down the three-quarter-mile-long dirt road that led into the narrow canyon, and he liked it that way. One of the residents was a snowbird and was gone for half the year, visiting family back in the Midwest, while the other was a retired school teacher who spent most of her long days doing plein air art near the San Juan River to the south.

The tourists who were drawn to the prehistoric ruins and canyons in this region stuck to the main attractions on the outskirts of town, and there were no established hiking trails or ATV routes behind Mercer's cabin. Anyone venturing to his place left telltale signs of their presence in the talcum-like sand on the road or in the memory cards of the numerous trailcams concealed around his land and the road.

The only time there was any excitement was when Luce chased off coyotes or when Mercer happened across mountain lion tracks near the propane tank off the rear of his cabin.

Once a week, Mercer walked into Blayne two miles away to get milk or bread from the local gas station, which also served as the grocery store, deli, hardware store, pizzeria and bakery in the town of two hundred and two souls.

Like him, the other residents valued their privacy and lived on an acre or two of high desert dotted with ancient cottonwood trees that provided the scant shade available in this otherwise parched landscape.

When he had moved here, he was told by a local archeologist that this area of southwestern Utah had a population of over fifty thousand people during the height of the prehistoric era around 1200 AD. He still frowned when thinking about that, since the only place to come anywhere near that figure now was Durango, Colorado, two hours to the east. Plus, Durango had snow and mountains and rivers and farmland to sustain a sizeable group of people, unlike the unforgiving terrain surrounding Blayne.

"Ready to go, girl?" he said, opening the door for Luce as she sprung up to the seat and sauntered over to the passenger's side, sitting at attention and inspecting the route ahead.

He climbed inside, stowing his pack on the rear bench seat and giving one last glance at the lashings securing the juniper table, convincing himself that he had properly anchored his precious cargo for the two-hour drive to Moab.

After meandering down the sinuous dirt road, he came to the two-lane highway, pausing at the bent stop sign whose base was entwined with Virginia creeper vines. Turning left, he drove for a half-mile then pulled into the Lazy J gas station to fill up his tank.

While fuel was cheaper in Moab, he preferred putting his money back into the few local businesses here, which teetered precariously upon a feast-or-famine income centered around seasonal tourism.

He rolled his windows down so Luce could hang her head out while he pumped the gas.

"You finally finished that hunk of wood?" said a voice from the entrance of the gas station. Mercer pivoted around, seeing Sheriff Arlo Dewey walking out with a Styrofoam cup of coffee and a chocolate-chip cookie, half out of its wrapper.

"Sure did. Taking her up to the owner's place finally."

"'Her.'" Dewey shook his head. "You artist types get too sentimental about your work. You gonna give *her* a big hug before you two part ways?"

Mercer chuckled. "And you law-enforcement types oughta think about seriously improving your diet."

Dewey smiled, biting off another piece of the brittle cookie. "This is just my brunch of sorts. Gotta have some sugar in me before I head down to the river to teach that swift-water rescue with the rest of our SAR group. Sure you can't make it?"

The sheriff was referring to the volunteer search-and-rescue unit comprised of locals. In addition to being one of three law-enforcement officers for the region and heading up the volunteer fire department, Dewey was also in charge of search and rescue.

Mercer shook his head. "Can't this time, but I'm still up for teaching the rappelling class at next month's meeting if that offer is still on."

"Heck, yeah," said Dewey. "The group's really excited about that...much more than hearing me blabber about how not to drown in the San Juan River."

Since he'd moved to Blayne, Mercer had made an early effort to befriend Dewey and his young deputies. He wanted them to know that he was friendly, easy-going and, most importantly, someone of use that they could rely on rather than being a mysterious hermit living at the end of an isolated road. The latter would only mean questions and internet queries, and while his cover story and alias were solid with a verifiable, if fictitious, online presence, the less people focused on him, the better.

Plus, his time on search and rescue had provided a means of learning all the travel routes in and out of the myriad canyons in the immense wilderness surrounding Blayne. In addition to his own multi-day treks with Luce, he had mapped out all the waterholes, springs and cave sites in a fifty-square-mile area behind his cabin.

Dewey put his dusty boot on the rear bumper just as the front door of the general store opened and out walked Angela Owens, the town's only redhead, a seasonal employee working as a mine surveyor for a private company out of Denver.

The woman took a sip of her coffee then looked up, freezing in her boots a few feet from the truck. Her repellent gaze at Mercer was enough to make Dewey pause chewing his cookie as he glanced back and forth between the two.

An audible sigh emerged from Mercer. "Angela," he said with a nod.

She smirked, narrowing her eyes, then turned towards Dewey, giving a faint smile. "Sheriff...good to see you."

Her smile suddenly turned authentic when she saw Luce, who was bobbing with excitement as she thrust her head out the open window, crying for Angela's attention.

The redhead shuffled closer, leaning her face in as Luce eagerly licked her chin and cheeks while Angela reciprocated with a neck scratch.

She angled her head briefly towards Mercer before staring back at Luce. "I hope he treats you better than the rest of the women in his life."

Before Angela strode away, she gave Mercer another frown then pivoted from the truck, walking to a weathered white Suburban with the logo for Palladium Industries on the side. She slowly backed up until she was inches from Mercer's front bumper then put it in drive and accelerated, spewing gravel onto the hood as she headed for the blacktop road.

"Wow, what have I missed these past few days?" said Dewey. "I thought you two were friends?" He held up one hand, clawing out air quotes at the latter term.

Mercer pulled out the gas nozzle, returning it to the pump. "She may be a little irritated that I haven't called her since we went out a couple nights ago."

"Does she know you don't own a phone?"

"I own a phone. I just keep it in my truck."

"Look, it's none of my business, but why don't you find your damn phone. Women take that communication stuff seriously, and you're gonna toss a hand-grenade into a relationship if you think otherwise. Though judging by her looks, you may be doing shrapnel removal at this point."

While Dewey yammered on about his marriage to his high-school sweetheart and the finer points of navigating communication quagmires with the opposite sex, Mercer watched the Suburban fade into the distance.

During the time he'd lived here, he had been content to fade into the background and just immerse himself in woodworking, hiking and occasional interactions during community events. Since most of the other residents in Blayne were either retirees or early twenty-somethings who came for the seasonal river-guide jobs, he had grown accustomed to being a loner.

Until he ventured into the café at the south end of town one morning two months ago, seeing a green-eyed beauty whose auburn hair seemed to illuminate the corner of the dining area.

She didn't notice him for the first few days, but that changed when he finally introduced himself after seeing she was intently reading *Dune*, one of his favorite books.

It had been a long time since he'd been with a woman. He loved everything about them...their walk, the way their hair smelled, and their eyes, which could either soothe or shred you, depending on the situation. Plus, Angela had been Luce-approved after that first meeting, and the wise dog could never be accused of lacking good judgement.

With Angela's nomadic job surveying old mines in San Juan County, he would only run into her a few times a week, but he could sense early on that they were heading into a slow-burn relationship. Or what Dewey had described as a "percolating friendship."

All of that changed earlier in the week when Angela spent the night at his cabin.

After Angela departed the following morning, he and Luce headed out on a long hike so he could sort through this new bend in the trail of his life in Blayne. When he returned, Mercer knew that he had to prevent his relationship with the alluring woman from going beyond their one encounter. Keeping his past hidden from someone he was clearly fond of was going to complicate his world in ways that would only spell trouble down the road.

Maybe it was his old demons coming back to paw at him, or the feeling that he would have to deceive someone else in his life, but either way, the cabin suddenly seemed too small, and he decided that his Zen routine of wood-working, hiking and reading was all he needed to sustain himself.

Mercer walked around to the other side of the truck

then leaned on the passenger's door, rubbing Luce's ears. "It'll be OK, girl. Angela's gonna be leavin' soon anyway once her job here is done."

Dewey tossed his empty coffee cup in the open trash barrel. "You know, if her job contract gets renewed, and it probably will, then she'll be back here next summer and maybe the next one after that. Heck, sometimes they even send folks down here during the winter on short-term projects."

Mercer frowned. "Don't you have jaywalking tickets to hand out to tourists?"

He shrugged his shoulders. "Nobody due in this week actually. All the hotel owners said they're dead bein' it's the weekend after Labor Day."

Mercer climbed into his truck. "Well, my bank account is gonna die if I don't get this table up to Moab."

Dewey gave a two-fingered salute then walked off towards his patrol car while Mercer pulled out of the gas station.

———

THE TRIP along Highway 95 went from bluff-colored mesas around Blayne to a slight uphill climb once he turned north onto Highway 191, passing through the Mormon towns of Blanding and Monticello before levelling off on the lonesome stretch of highway heading towards Moab.

Most of the tourists, mountain bikers and Jeep enthusiasts in Moab came from Salt Lake City, so the route from the north end was far more congested, allowing him the luxury of letting his mind wander along the buttes and distant mountains.

Still, with each monthly trip to Moab to deliver his

custom furniture and obtain his mail from a UPS store, he was astounded at the constant sprawl infiltrating the formerly sleepy town.

While the *Welcome to Moab* sign along the highway announced the local population as being 5317, which was roughly five thousand people more than Blayne, Mercer felt like Moab doubled in size at every visit given the burgeoning rash of second homes whose owners were out of Salt Lake or Denver.

After arriving at the south side of town and contending with three consecutive red lights, he was already pining for Blayne.

"Man, have I grown soft, Luce. Bangkok, Johannesburg and Tel Aviv traffic is a hundred times worse than what we have in this country." He patted her on the neck. "Bet you never heard me say that before on these trips." She only flicked her head to the right, baring her teeth slightly as a duo of Pomeranians bounced along the sidewalk, tethered to their plump owner's waist.

But on each trip to Moab, he still scanned and watched and observed everyone. Those on the streets, on their bikes, in his rearview mirror. Anything that seemed out of place or anyone who aroused his suspicions, indicating that they were more than gawking tourists. While the old habits of intense situational awareness never died, he had to make sure that they never got rusty, and the crowds in Moab were about his only means of practicing.

THE DELIVERY of the table went smoothly, with the owner's teenage son helping Mercer hoist it from the pickup and place it in the spacious kitchen of the two-story cliffside home. A few words about the care and maintenance of the wood along with a colorful backstory on the nature of the juniper's origins and the transaction was nearly complete.

The client, a balding man with wire-rimmed glasses, removed eight one-hundred-dollar bills from his money clip, then both men parted with handshakes.

Mercer only did cash. Even back in Blayne, his fuel, food and supplies were all paid for in currency. He pocketed seven of the bills, saving the last for some new jigsaw blades and varnish at the hardware store.

It was on the return trip through Moab after purchasing his items and retrieving his mail that he saw the black SUV in his rearview mirror as it followed him south along the main strip. The driver was the same lanky man he'd seen sitting outside at the café across from the UPS store earlier.

"Jaguar F-PACE...that's a pretty fancy rental vehicle, son. You ain't local. You just arrive from Salt Lake?" He spoke aloud, his windows up and the air on as Luce curled into a ball on the front seat, her afternoon nap overdue.

With only a few blocks of downtown in sight before the long stretch of monotonous blacktop heading south, he slowed and made a right turn then went west for three blocks and turned right again. He pulled into a curbside parking spot outside a life-insurance office, putting his phone to his ear and pretending he was searching the building for the address.

A second later, he caught a glimpse of the SUV in his rearview mirror as it paused briefly at the last intersection before continuing west out of sight.

Mercer resumed driving down the street, making another right, hoping his suspicions were off and that the driver was just another misguided tourist.

Venturing back onto the main road, he headed back

towards Blayne on Highway 191, driving past a Maverick gas station, Wyndham Hotel and later an RV park.

It wasn't until he left the fringes of town and was back in the high desert that his pulse quickened at the distant black image in his rearview mirror.

CHAPTER 2

WITH THE BLACK SUV appearing nearly twelve miles outside of Moab, he knew the driver was keeping an unusual amount of space between them. That meant he wasn't working solo and had another vehicle on the road ahead or Mercer's vehicle was bugged.

It could have happened at any of the places he'd stopped to shop.

Maybe I've let my guard down too much. He'd always known that his former career in the CIA's Special Activities Division was sure to have drawn a long list of people who wanted to see his head on a pike.

Is the Agency after my ass for their money...or is Rohrbach looking for the diamonds? Those were the two names at the top of that list, and both had considerable motives and resources to hunt him down. He'd been meticulous in creating his new identity and life in the hinterlands of the Four Corners region, but the tail on him now indicated that something had gone awry.

Regardless, he needed to gain the tactical advantage, and that meant getting off this highway. Mercer drove south for another three miles then turned onto a narrow dirt road that headed east through miles of Forest Service land. He had been mule deer hunting up this way and had camped out long enough to get a feel for the tangle of jeep trails that wound along the edges of the arroyos.

Hitting the bumpy road caused Luce to spring up, glancing first at him in surprise then out at the windows.

"You're gonna come with me, girl. Hopefully, this won't take long."

He drove for another mile then slowed, turning onto a road choked with willows on the right side where a tiny stream was flowing.

Two hundred yards ahead, he pulled off onto the shoulder on the left, crunching over spent beer cans and the remnants of some charred branches from an old campfire. The space was big enough for three vehicles and was a parking area for locals venturing up to the cliff dwellings that dotted the limestone ridge running parallel to the stream.

He had been here with Angela a few weeks ago when he insisted on showing her around the area, since she'd only arrived in Blayne in mid-July.

Mercer removed his backpack from the rear seat, pulling out the three 15-round magazines for the Glock 17 concealed in a holster under his baggy t-shirt then motioned for Luce to jump out. He walked around the chassis and rear wheels on both sides, dropping to one knee on the right side. His eyes narrowed as he gazed at a magnetic GPS device attached to the wheel well.

"Dammit."

He left it in place for now. Mercer stood up, locking the doors then trot-walking up the steep trail that snaked towards the rim of the shallow canyon, weaving through a tangle of box elders, making sure to stop every twenty feet and leave obvious boot tracks in the dirt. When he arrived at the rim, Luce paused beside his leg as he glanced to the south, seeing a plume of dust along the road he'd just driven.

"Here he comes in that fancy Jag."

Mercer pivoted, briskly walking along the canyon's edge for a few minutes then dropping below the rim again onto a deer trail. A short scramble later, he was at the bottom of the arroyo again. He nestled into a clump of willows, Luce giving him a perplexed look at the nature of their horse-shoe-shaped jaunt.

While he had trained Luce in verbal commands he had recalled seeing military K-9 handlers use in the past, he now reverted solely to hand signals.

There was just enough of a curve in the canyon at this point that he and the dog would be concealed in the sparse foliage while still being able to glimpse the path ahead.

The SUV slowly crept down the road, pulling in near his F-150. The man who exited was the same one from the café in Moab. Dressed in a short-sleeved polo shirt and khaki pants, he looked like someone who had just stepped out of an Eddie Bauer catalog.

The man had short-cropped blond hair and an athletic build, and Mercer was sure he could see a slight bulge from a concealed pistol under the man's shirt near the beltline.

He had seen enough hitmen and hired guns like this one before to know that only one of them would leave this canyon alive. Mercer watched him move towards the trail, searching for tracks then repeatedly gazing at the rim.

Hugging the willows, Nick let the sound of the stream cover his passage along the dry ground, making his way towards his pickup. Luce crept alongside him as she had done before on big-game hunts. He removed his Glock, keeping it at a low-ready as he scanned the road for anything that could betray his approach.

Arriving at his Ford, he could see the man removing a pair of binoculars and his iPhone from the Jag then closing the door.

Mercer used the commotion to slowly stalk between the vehicles. As the man signed off from whomever he'd briefly spoken with, Mercer stepped out, pointing his weapon at the back of the man's head.

"Just stay put unless you want your brains painting the rocks." He scrutinized the man's clothing and ankles, searching for the outline of other weapons. "Who sent you?"

The man remained silent, slowly lowering the binoculars onto the hood of the vehicle then letting his arms hang by his sides instead of raising them. He subtly unlocked his knees, lowering his center of gravity.

Mercer steadied his grip. "I've only ever known two quick-draw guys who thought they could pull off the move you're about to try. One is dead, and the other one enjoys spoon-fed meals."

The man turned his head slightly. "It's taken a long time to find you."

Nick canted his head after hearing the South African accent with its subtle hint of Dutch. "You one of Edgar Rohrbach's guys...is that what this is about?"

The man gave a faint nod, glancing over his shoulder as he shifted his weight again.

"How did you find me? And keep your fucking hands still."

"The name Hassan mean anything? He was killed during an INTERPOL raid on his place last spring...but that encrypted hard-drive of his survived, and Rohrbach has a lot of contacts around the world."

Mercer's right eye twitched. He thought back to his meeting with Omar Hassan in Kuala Lumpur five years ago, when the trusted forger had procured a series of new passports and travel documents for him. He had watched Hassan delete Mercer's files upon completion of the forgeries, but it seemed the man had a backup hard-drive that contained the information. Hassan must have cracked during the INTERPOL interrogation and made a deal in exchange for selling out his clients. Regardless, the man before him now meant that Mercer's cover story and carefully constructed life in Utah were blown.

"You know, you could make this easy and just point me to those three red diamonds that you walked off with five years ago. I'll forget I ever saw you."

"Not sure what the hell you're referring to, but the Rohrbachs have only ever been interested in lining their own pockets at the expense of whatever African nation they are plundering."

"Edgar expanded the family holdings in Africa and has considerable resources, so if you think that this is going to end here in this land of cowpies, you're gravely mistaken. Your days...your hours are numbered."

He knew the man was stalling while a backup team was probably enroute.

Mercer was growing impatient as he saw the man's slight arm movement again. "You know the thing that is going to piss me off the most about shooting you?"

"Gettin' your hands bloody again?"

"No, the indecency of scaring my dog."

The man kicked dirt back with his boot then pivoted.

His left hand lifted his shirt while the right reached for the concealed pistol.

Mercer's Glock barked out a single round, which struck the man's left temple, the body falling forward into a clump of cactus near the trail.

Out of habit, Mercer glanced up at the surrounding ridges then down either side of the road for any movement. He moved up to the dead man, removing an HK pistol then locating the cellphone in his pants pocket.

Mercer walked back to his F-150, kneeling down, motioning for Luce, who had darted under his vehicle.

She crept out, skulking towards him as he rested his hand upon her back. "Looks like it's time to say goodbye to Blayne."

CHAPTER 3

HE REMEMBERED it mostly in fragments. That's how traumatic events worked. The mind compartmentalizes horror and tragedy until it can cope with bite-sized pieces over the ensuing years.

What isn't confronted head on is pushed down deep until it eventually reaches the jagged line of the soul, only emerging in sweat-soaked nightmares that threaten to shatter one's carefully constructed walls.

That was how he always recalled his last days in Liberia. Though it was only five years ago, Mercer pictured himself as much younger and a little less jaded. Such afterthought never helped to squelch the nightmares.

Back then, he went by the name of Nathan Hendrix. And he felt assured that the work he was doing for the CIA in West Africa was worth the cost. Sometimes he even caught himself thinking it was noble, if training indigenous Gola tribesmen in counter-insurgency could be called such a thing.

After two years of instructing the natives in the rugged jungle highlands of northwestern Liberia that bordered

Guinea, Hendrix and fellow CIA agent Deacon Crowe had succeeded in creating a strong army of resistance fighters to quell the government forces led by President Kananga, who resided in the capital city of Monrovia along the coast.

While Mercer had little comprehension of what went on in Washington D.C. to warrant his presence in Liberia, his case officer was clear on his instructions: prevent Kananga's forces from controlling the diamond-rich highlands along the northern border until a U.S. cooperative regime could be installed in Monrovia.

Two years later, the training of his resistance fighters throughout the surrounding mountain ranges was complete, and Hendrix's departure from Africa was imminent. Except a deadly villain without geographic boundaries suddenly emerged when Ebola swept through the coastal cities, ravaging the country. During the resulting shutdowns and the death of President Kananga and many of his advisors, a mercenary army believed to be supported by billionaire diamond broker Edgar Rohrbach, who sought to control diamond mining in West Africa, flooded in through the porous borders of Sierra Leone at a time when the surrounding region was a cauldron of chaos.

Initially, Hendrix was at a loss to explain the devastating turn of events until he realized that Crowe had sold out to Rohrbach.

Mercer could still smell the charred grass huts and hear the screams in the village where he was living when the first mortars pounded the hillside, the enemy knowing exactly where to strike.

His efforts and the noble work of his warrior-tribesmen were reduced to flames and rubble in hours after the first of dozens of barrages upon the ancient villages that dotted the mountains. He and the remaining fighters and their families were on the run for weeks, fleeing on foot towards Guinea while being hunted by Rohrbach's mercenaries flooding through the countryside as they tried to eliminate any witnesses to their atrocities.

With his agency contacts going silent and Liberia collapsing into a failed nation, Hendrix used his remaining CIA funds to bribe border guards to ensure the safe passage of the surviving families into neighboring Guinea.

Three weeks later, he received a message on an old email account about a dead-drop in a city park in Conraky, a coastal city in western Guinea. There was no information on who sent the terse dispatch but he suspected it was from Neil Patterson, his former training officer at Langley.

Burn Notice. Go Deep. Be Safe.

With his finances inaccessible, he needed funds to begin a new life, and his options were severely limited. There was no way he was going to reach out to old friends or contacts and risk their lives.

Then he remembered.

While the Rohrbach-funded mercenaries led by Crowe knew exactly where to strike the Liberian native villages, Hendrix also had intimate knowledge of Rohrbach's diamond smuggling routes through the mountains.

Ten days later, after he and a handful of his native Gola friends struck one of the numerous small convoys in a remote jungle valley near the Sierra Leone border, Hendrix had enough raw diamonds for his needs as well as providing for his men and their families back in Guinea.

But what he hadn't counted on was the discovery of a small strong-box containing three ruby-red diamonds. He had heard rumor of such rare gemstones, and he certain that the mine foreman, an honorable man whom Mercer had known, had probably been safekeeping the diamonds for transport to the Ministry of the Interior in the capital.

Hendrix wasn't a broker, but even he knew that each of the grape-sized diamonds would probably be worth 20 million dollars or more. But any attempt to sell them on the black market would paint another bullseye on his back alongside the one he was sure to already have from the CIA.

Now, five years later, as Mercer looked up at the cobalt Utah sky, he knew the past had found him.

And a tidal wave of violence was about to engulf his life again.

CHAPTER 4

MERCER SEARCHED the front of the vehicle then the back seat, where he found a black windbreaker whose back bore the FBI logo. He thought of the implications. Either Rohrbach had infiltrated an American law-enforcement agency and Mercer had just killed a federal agent, or this guy had obtained some falsified credentials.

He surmised the latter was most likely the case, but it still impressed upon him the lengths to which Rohrbach would go to obtain the red diamonds.

After he finished sifting through the vehicle, removing a tablet and a shoulder bag, Mercer dragged the limp body into the willow thicket by the stream.

He returned to his Ford, plucking out the GPS device from under his wheel well and putting it on the driver's seat next to Luce. When he was done, he scanned the man's cell-phone, seeing a text message from fifteen minutes ago.

Be at your location in thirty minutes.

"Does that mean here or at my place in Blayne? Either way, that doesn't leave much time."

He surmised it had to be the present location, as the

sender was most likely basing their message on the dead man's GPS coordinates.

Mercer walked back to the dead man's SUV, putting the phone inside then returning to his own vehicle. Then he and Luce sped north for three miles, emerging on a different dirt road. At the intersection of an old jeep route, he stepped out, flinging the GPS tracker into the brush.

He weighed the options: driving northeast and crossing into Colorado and leaving Blayne behind for good or risking the trip south to his cabin and quickly gathering some critical items before disappearing onto the Navajo Reservation for a while until he could determine his next move.

He needed to get back to his cabin in Blayne to retrieve some items. During his time there, he had always been careful not to have a heavy footprint of personal items scattered about his small abode. While his truck was equipped like a rolling survival warehouse with numerous bug-out supplies, he needed access to the cyber-intrusion software on his laptop to see if he could crack the firewall on the tablet and pick up any intel on his pursuers.

With his passports and other fake IDs blown, he'd have to obtain new credentials, and that would probably mean heading down into Mexico.

NINETY MINUTES LATER, he made the turn-off to his cabin. The only tracks on the road were from his truck's earlier passage and the narrow tires of a mountain bike, which he was sure belonged to Aaron Rhodes, the high schooler painting his neighbor's house. He sped down the road, seeing the mountain bike parked beside Jessica's place. He figured she was somewhere in the backcountry doing her plein air artwork for the day.

He sped up, continuing ahead to his cabin. After hastily parking, Mercer got out and trotted up the steps, leaving his truck door open so Luce could follow.

The dog sauntered to her water and food dishes, partaking of one then the other before jumping up on the small couch in the living room.

Mercer set down the tablet on his desk. He opened the second drawer on the right, removing a false bottom of stained plywood then placing his thumb over the biometric lock on the safe. When the metal lid sprung open, he removed his laptop, turning it on then plugging in the tablet.

While his code-breaking software went to work on the dead man's device, he ran to the back closet, yanking out the mop and cleaning supplies then removing a pane of faux paneling at the rear. He retrieved a large backpack that contained his primary evasion items for a three-day trek: MREs, water, medical supplies, sleeping and shelter gear, and a takedown MK12 rifle equipped with a nightvision scope and a suppressor contained in a side compartment. Beneath those items was a flat zippered satchel with his now-useless passports, a thousand dollars in cash, and a small leather pouch with a dozen raw diamonds. He removed the passports, tossing them back into the hidden compartment in the wall.

A beeping noise emitted from his computer, and he leaned the pack down against his desk, scanning the contents of the tablet. There were only two files.

One was a GPS tracking display. He clicked on it, seeing a static signal where he had killed his pursuer south of

Moab. The other two red dots were moving in unison south on Highway 191, directly towards Blayne.

"Dammit. That's only thirty minutes from here."

He glanced out at his truck then the road beyond for any signs that the sheriff or Feds were coming.

They could already be setting up roadblocks around town, especially since they're posing as Feds and may have notified Dewey and his guys. Or there could be a shit-ton of guys on their way from the south so they can bottle up every road out of here.

The last thing he needed was a high-speed chase through miles of open terrain where he'd have no tactical advantage or means of escape. Nor did he want any harm to come to Dewey or his two deputies or any locals.

Right now, he knew his only option was buying time and distance from the coming manhunters, which meant Plan B, evading on foot through the canyons out back until he could get to the San Juan River, eleven miles to the south. With the roadless wilderness adjacent to his cabin, he'd at least have a fighting chance of escaping.

He clicked on the other file, his own image filling the screen. Mercer grabbed the edge of the desk like he was holding on to a lifeline as he stared into his face.

He recalled the day it was taken by a native friend during his last six months in Liberia. He was much leaner then and more tan from years of living in the jungle.

If I could only go back in time and tell you about the horrors that were about to unfold. Maybe your life and the lives of so many others would have turned out differently.

He didn't have time to linger on the past. He needed to get on the move in the daylight that remained.

Mercer disconnected the tablet cord then tapped on the security feed for the dozen trailcams and video devices he had peppered throughout his property and along the dirt road.

The only thing that showed up was Aaron Rhodes hauling a paint canister out from Jessica's shed. He watched the young man for a second then glanced at Luce.

He held up his hand, motioning for the dog to follow, both of them hopping into his truck. He sped down the lane to his neighbor's house, stepping out and leaving the door open for Luce to follow as he headed to the rear where Aaron was atop a ladder, painting the eaves.

"Hey, Mr. Mercer, how are you?"

"Great, Aaron, thanks. Say, could you do me a huge favor? A couple of friends of mine are in town, and we're all gonna go on a long hike along Badger Gulch. I was wondering if you could drive my truck down to the trailhead parking area on the other side of the gulch so we can just drive back to their car rather than having to return the way we came."

The scruffy teen stepped down from the ladder, peering into the living room window. "I told Ms. Greeney that I'd finish this up by early afternoon so she didn't have the paint fumes coming through her windows all night, but I've only got about an hour of work left, so it shouldn't be a problem."

"It'll only take twenty minutes. You can throw your bike in the truck and ride back here in no time." He reached into his wallet, removing a fifty dollar bill. "Maybe this will help. You can put it towards that new compound bow you've been telling me about.

"Wow, heck yeah, thanks."

Mercer tossed him the keys. "If you could head over there now, that'd be great. Just like to know everything is all set before our trip."

The kid placed his paint can and brush on the plastic

dropcloth then wiped his hands on the front of his jeans. "You got it. Have fun out there."

Mercer nodded, knowing that the only fun in his life had been in the last few months leading up to this day.

He knelt down next to Luce, leaning his forehead against hers and whispering to her softly like the day he first brought her home as a pup.

When he was done, he glanced back up at Aaron, who was taking a swig of water from the garden hose.

"One more thing. Can you let Jessica know that I had to leave Luce here? It's going to be too rough a hike for her."

"Sure."

Mercer pulled her close for one last hug as the dog licked his chin, then he escorted her in through the rear door of the house, giving her the hand motion to stay. He felt his insides splintering apart as he looked into her trusting eyes, but he knew the rugged canyons ahead with their cactus, boulders and possible rappels would be too risky for her given the frenetic pace at which he'd need to travel.

He also knew after today, he'd no longer be Nick Mercer, and that he'd be a man on the run again, probably for the rest of his days, assuming he lived beyond the next twenty-four hours.

That would hinge on how far he managed to get on foot before sundown.

CHAPTER 5

ONE HOUR LATER, Deacon Crowe stepped from his black SUV in the parking lot for the Badger Gulch trailhead, donning the FBI vest that he grabbed from the open hatch in back. When he was done adjusting the vest straps and squinching down the tight-fitting brimmed hat, he scanned the two dozen vehicles and a white RV in the opposite corner.

His second-in-command, Jake Atley, moved up alongside him. The man grabbed a water bottle from the back then liberally sprinkled it on a green bandanna, wiping it along his reddened face.

"Fuck, how can it be this hot here in September?" Atley said.

"You'll be back in an air-conditioned jet by day's end, so quit complaining and take the rest of the team and search around the vehicles."

He and his eight-man team had been driving around the small town, searching for Mercer's truck since the man had evidently ditched the GPS tracking device after killing one of Crowe's advance scouts south of Moab.

He instructed his men to avoid speaking with the locals about their search and, if pressed about their presence in the region, to indicate that there was an escaped fugitive who was on the run through the Four Corners area.

Crowe didn't want the tiny town to go into full lockdown and create panic, which would only create interest with the outlying law-enforcement agencies and raise too many red flags as to why the Feds had descended upon the region without notifying them.

He grabbed a water bottle from the back hatch, pouring some on his hand then rubbing it along several crimson splotches on his tan shirt sleeve, shoving back the memory of violently abducting two FBI agents in Durango whose dead bodies were now lying in a deep gorge.

As Rohrbach's off-the-books field operations leader, Crowe had decided that having official cover as federal agents was the only way to circumvent the local authorities and apprehend his subject with minimal interference from the miniscule population.

His earpiece crackled, a woman's voice coming over the comms. "Our satellite imagery around Blayne is spotty, but the truck you had me backtrack out of Moab should be in that parking lot towards the north side beyond the RV."

"Copy that. So he came right here after he dispatched my guy?"

"Mmm...looks like he made one stop down a dirt road near Blayne, but the trees are too thick to tell what's there."

"Keep scouring the area adjacent to the parking lot and see if you can locate a lone individual on foot whom I'm guessing is probably not going to be sticking to the trails."

Deacon signed off then motioned to the four nearby men to begin glassing the areas beyond the trailhead. While his mercenaries were all skilled manhunters, trying to locate signs of Mercer amidst throngs of tourist tracks was going to be a challenge and would bog down their timeline.

He heard the gravel substrate near the entrance crunching and turned to see a sheriff's vehicle pulling up. Crowe told his men to continue searching while he made a beeline for the white-and-green SUV adorned with the San Juan County sheriff's logo.

The officer inside parked then got out, donning a weathered white cowboy hat and walking towards Crowe. "Something going on that I should know about?"

"Name's Deacon Crowe, Durango Office." He extended a hand as the two men shook. "My apologies for not contacting you sooner, Sheriff Dewey," he said without looking at the man's name badge. "We didn't think our manhunt would take us down here. Figured this would stay up north, but the guy we're after killed one of my men, and we got word that his truck was found down here."

Dewey glanced at the other agents moving between vehicles at the end of the lot. "Should I be worried? I mean, we have a number of tourists and backpackers out on the trails around here. If there's a dangerous criminal on the run then I should have been informed already."

Crowe was about to answer when one of his men came up beside him, whispering in his ear. The black man's unusually thick accent made Dewey take notice.

Crowe thrust his chin towards a dusty Ford F-150 at the opposite end of the lot. "Looks like this is a false lead. The owner of that RV down there said the driver was some kid who dropped the vehicle off then headed out on his mountain bike."

Dewey craned his head. "That's Nick Mercer's rig. He lives in a cabin not far from here. What's he got to do with this?"

"He's the fugitive we're after."

"What? How's that?"

Crowe pulled out his iPhone, showing an image of a scruffy man with a weary expression. "This is from a few years ago. Is this the guy you know?"

Dewey licked his lip, giving a slow nod.

"And he was up in Moab today?" said Crowe.

"Yeah. So?"

"He's been a wanted fugitive for years, living under numerous aliases. We finally got a break on his whereabouts recently. Thought we would wrap him up after he left Moab, but instead he led one of my guys down an isolated canyon then shot him in the back of the skull like an animal."

Dewey's cheek twitched. He put his hands on his duty belt, shaking his head. "You say Nick Mercer did that? You must have the wrong guy. I know him. Nick's not a killer."

Crowe grinned. "You have no idea what a predator this guy is, Sheriff." He patted the man on the shoulder. "Why don't you take me down to this cabin of his. We can talk more, and I can fill you in on the feral dog who's been living in your little community all this time."

CHAPTER 6

AFTER LEAVING Luce at his neighbor's place, Mercer trotted back to his cabin. Out of habit, he kept glancing to his right side where Luce would be keeping pace. The return trip seemed to last an hour, and he kept gazing back down the road, knowing the cattle dog was probably watching him from a window.

Focus. You have time and distance to worry about now.

He returned to the back closet, this time removing a gallon jug of muriatic acid from the cleaning shelf. He had originally bought it to strip the old sealer off the sandstone flooring in his kitchen when he bought the place.

He went to the sink, putting a metal stopper on the right drain then carefully pouring in the remains of the noxious fluid, making sure not to splash any on his skin.

When he was done, he returned to his desk, unplugging his laptop and submersing it in the acid.

Next, he grabbed his backpack and the small shoulder bag and headed to the back door.

Mercer plucked a one-liter bottle of water from a small table, quickly swigging it down, making his stomach into an auxiliary water container. Given his earlier consumption of water, he knew he would be fully hydrated for at least the next ninety minutes or so as he headed up the narrow canyon with his heavy pack.

He had mentally planned out this exodus for years, initially hoping to rely on a mountain bike or dirt bike, but the trails were too steep and the canyons too numerous to navigate with a heavy load, and he adjusted his evasion plans to suit a hasty hike on foot.

Darting out the back door, he trotted to the old cattle fencing that delineated his property from the millions of acres of federal land to the west. Pausing at the rickety gate, he glanced back at his tiny cabin and the back porch where he'd spent many nights gazing up at the stars. His four peaceful years in Blayne now felt like a brief respite from his time operating in war-torn regions of the world, and he wondered what would come of his life after today.

Mercer crossed onto BLM land, heading along a deer trail that he had gone running on daily, only this time burdened by a sixty-five-pound pack, which made for slower going. While he had to gain distance quickly, he also had to pace himself for the rugged landscape ahead. A wrong step or a slip on a rock would mean a sprained ankle or a busted hip, and his trek would be over.

He had to follow the gently rising slope that led to the mesa ahead then go another half mile until he came across the beginning of where Black Canyon and Gould Canyon began. Those were two finger canyons that were a mile apart but ran parallel for eleven miles, eventually ending at the San Juan River.

While he had traveled in and around both canyons over the years, he preferred Gould, which had a sandy bottom and fewer boulders. But today he would travel along the rim of Black Canyon then descend into its recesses at the halfway point, since there were far more areas for conceal-ment within its many caves and old mineshafts.

There was also one forty-foot vertical rock chute in Black Canyon, and his pack contained climbing rope and a harness to negotiate that hazardous stretch. Three miles later, he had a sixty-foot rappel straight down a vertical slick-rock chute. After that, the remaining mileage was along the gravel-strewn bottom until the mouth of the canyon opened into the San Juan River. As a contingency, his alternate route was to head cross-country towards Gould Canyon, but that gorge had a sandy drainage with too many exposed areas and was only considered as a last resort.

He did both routes twice a year to refamiliarize himself with the terrain, to time his progress and to resupply the three hidden caches along the way. His time with search and rescue had taught him the challenges of the region, and over the years, he found himself committing the topographic maps on his living room wall to memory.

Once he made it to the San Juan River, the next phase of evasion would begin, but he hoped by then his pursuers would be hampered by the maze of mountains and arroyos in the region—or dead, either at the hands of the wilds or his own, if necessary.

He preferred the former but had examined enough chokepoints along this route before to turn the landscape into a formidable weapon.

CHAPTER 7

"READ ABOUT YOU, Sheriff. Your reputation precedes you," said Crowe as he and Dewey walked from their vehicles up to Mercer's cabin.

"Oh, how's that?"

"'The lawman that no one could corrupt'...isn't that what they say about you?"

Dewey hadn't heard that phrase in years. It was a slogan that was more of a curse than a blessing, connected with a case twenty years ago as a young patrolman when he turned in Blayne's own sheriff for covering up a murder case.

He frowned. "That was a long time ago when I was just out of the academy and had come back here as a new deputy."

"So, you're saying you're corruptible now?" He chuckled, patting Dewey on the arm as the older man shook his head, giving a confused expression.

"Walk with me, Sheriff. I need to get into this fugitive's head, so whatever you can tell me about his lifestyle, habits, favorite haunts—anything you think would help us track him down—would be of great help."

They progressed around the cabin, Crowe pausing every few feet to stare inside Mercer's toolshed, detached garage, or up at the tawny ridges, occasionally emitting a faint grin before he slung another barrage of questions at Dewey.

The sheriff glanced at the tight FBI vest, which seemed shrink-wrapped to the man. "Look, Agent Crowe, I've worked with Nick on search and rescue. He's a solid guy and has been instrumental in saving a lot of lives during his time here. Plus, he's really helped out our community. Are you sure you've got the right guy?"

Crowe put his hands on his hips as they paused under the shade of a cottonwood tree near the back porch. "How many people you got in this *town*?"

"Just over two hundred, depending on the time of year. Half that in winter."

"I imagine in a place like this, the day-to-day involves handling the occasional drunk tourist or maybe some kids getting out of hand with graffiti." He glanced up at a passing cumulus cloud blotting out the sun. "I'm not in any way trying to diminish your work or this town, but in my experience, when a place is lacking an ugly underbelly like you'd see in Phoenix or L.A., people are far more trusting. And in a place like Blayne, professional criminals like Mercer would find it easy to prey upon the good folks you've got here."

"How do you mean, 'professional criminal'? What's he wanted for anyway?"

"Let's just say that Nick Mercer spilled a lot of blood in Africa when he worked as a hired gun. The man committed atrocities that made even my stomach churn...from what I learned about him from INTERPOL."

Crowe removed his sunglasses, heading to the back porch as Dewey's mouth hung open. "How about we talk inside, Sheriff. You might want to be sitting down for what I'm about to tell you."

CHAPTER 8

FOR THE PAST forty minutes since he'd left his cabin, Mercer had maintained a brisk pace, alternating between trotting along open stretches on the game trail and walking through the overgrown sections on the mesa.

From his years of working with counter-insurgents in Africa, he knew that time and distance were his only allies right now. In addition to his own field experience, he had once taken a personal interest in escape and evasion stories, ranging from the Apaches during the tumultuous years of the Geronimo campaign to prison escapees and downed combat pilots on the run in hostile territory.

Mercer discovered one thing that all successful evaders had in common: superb aerobic capacity. Simply, they kept moving, often at a slow trot, to get outside of the search radius of their pursuers. The Hollywood notion of pausing to set up an elaborate mantrap that hoisted a pursuer off the ground or sent them into an earthen pit with spikes was absurd, unless an evader had considerable time, sweat, tools and know-how to construct such things.

Given his four-mile daily runs, punching-bag workouts

in his toolshed and his woodworking vocation, he kept reasonably fit. He also had the added advantage of knowing the terrain ahead, having spent the past few years on countless treks with Luce.

But he also knew that things had changed in the technology realm since he left active fieldwork, and he surmised that his pursuers were probably well funded and had the latest portable drones, satellite imagery and thermal devices to aid in the chase.

And since Rohrbach is behind this, his guys will be some hardened mercenaries.

He glanced up, watching two ravens circling above the steep canyon walls as the familiar aroma of young cottonwoods and tamarisk trees to his right gave him some sense of comfort that the mercs on his trail were most likely unfamiliar with the extensive maze of canyons in this sparsely populated region.

As he picked up his pace, Mercer ran through the topographic map in his head of the nearby arroyos and mesas, recalling the chokepoints, shortcuts, waterholes and vast stretches of slickrock that would impede a pursuer.

"Let's see if we can't make this place work to our advantage." Habitually, he glanced down to his right, expecting Luce to be staring back at him, her pointy ears flicking and her eyes fixed on him as she interpreted his facial expressions and body language.

Then he realized his only companions were the ravens above.

A part of him felt a pang of loss, but the nomadic side of his psyche chided him for being so attached to the dog. He'd spend nearly all of his adult life floating from place to place, first with the military then with the Agency. He had lived out of his backpack for so long that it felt like another appendage. And despite the cabin's rustic location, settling into Blayne seemed unnatural...a tether to a modern world he wanted nothing to do with.

Then came Luce...and recently Angela Owens. The surveyor's arrival in Blayne ignited a spark for close companionship that he'd kept submerged for years.

He shook his head at the short-lived relationship with the headstrong woman.

Time to let it all go...again. Time to push on. And keep pushing on. The trail ahead is all that matters now.

He crested a small hill, hugging the juvenile pines and junipers. Arriving at the top, he squatted to avoid silhouetting himself against the cobalt sky. From here, he had a three-hundred-sixty-degree view of the valley and the route he had just taken. Mercer removed his small tablet, gazing back towards the faint outline of his cabin roof through the sycamores and cottonwoods.

He tapped on the settings feature, enabling it to connect to one of the two cell towers near Blayne. He pulled out a small device, attaching it to a side port, which would create a personal hotspot. This might be the last time he would have the reception to tap into his home security feed.

Entering his password, he scanned through the trailcam and video feed images, seeing Dewey's distinctive white cowboy hat as he walked alongside another man.

Mercer's eyes widened, his stomach coiling in knots.

"Shit. Deacon Crowe." He gazed up at the sky for a second. "Of course you're involved in this, you son of a bitch."

His calm detachment melted away as a bitter taste flooded his mouth. A barrage of images from clandestine missions throughout Africa with Crowe raced across his mind. Only then, they were more naive, and certainly idealistic about what Langley was trying to accomplish with their foreign policy.

He knew the man's presence in Blayne meant it was more than just about fulfilling a contract for Rohrbach.

This was also personal.

Now, Mercer just hoped there would come a time when he could dial in his rifle sights on Crowe's head.

CHAPTER 9

IT WAS LATE AFTERNOON, and the wind on Owl Mesa had kicked up, sending every fleck of dust and pollen into the sun-beaten faces of the two-man work crew squatting with their trowels over the faint outline of a boarded up vertical mineshaft entrance near a clump of pinon pine trees.

"This is one of the early designs, given the way the rock is stacked around the edges and the lack of long-term living sites in the area, most likely from around the 1890s," said Angela Owens as she pulled her thin scarf up around her nose until the blast of wind ceased.

Beside her, Thomas Kapp, a tall man in white pants and a blue jacket, coughed repeatedly before taking a swig of water from his bottle. "God, there's so much history out here. It's incredible, isn't it?"

"Just wait until you spend time with the archeologist for this region...then you'll get to see just how many cliff dwellings and rock-art panels are hidden throughout these canyons."

Owens tried her best to remain calm while answering his questions, since the man was the director of the new visitor center in Blayne, and she'd promised Dewey that she'd show Kapp a few of the prominent historic sites in the region that tourists were sure to ask about.

"So this mineshaft and the others you drove me around to yesterday were all related to a particular mining firm, or were they all just lone-wolf prospectors?"

"A little of both, actually. The larger firms weren't active around here, although they may have laid down some mining claims and done some digging for a while to see if there was anything worth a return." She waved her hand towards the ridges of slickrock to the west. "This particular geologic layer wasn't exactly known for its mineral wealth, but there were the occasional veins of silver or copper to be found."

She needed to keep playing the educator and hold back her usual sarcasm, hoping the man would get his fill of windblown sand in the face and want to depart for his return drive back to the comfort of his office in Blayne. Her official job title was safety inspector for Palladium Industries, examining old mining sites to determine if they posed a hazard or health risk, and she still had sixty-one more sites left to survey if she was going to fulfill her three-month assignment in San Juan County.

Just finish jotting down your damn notes and be on your way so I can get back to my damn survey.

He took another swig of water, glancing down at her bare ring finger. "This must be a lonely life for a woman...on the road or in the wilds all the time. Is there a Mr. Owens?"

Angela had endured the past two days of Kapp's sideways glances at her body and his not-so-subtle chauvinism, and she momentarily considered shoving him onto the clump of prickly-pear cactus to his rear.

She heard one of her local workers chuckle and say

something to the other man but only made out the words *Mercer* and *commitment issues*, informing her that their fling had probably made it into the Blayne newspaper.

Angela tried to push back her frustration at Mercer's sudden aloofness since their night together, wondering why the man had slammed a door in her face without any explanation.

She had thought of continuing to pursue Mercer immediately following their short interlude to see if he came around...hell, there weren't a lot of choices in Blayne, she told herself, but she found it a Sisyphean task to break through his emotional barriers, finding it much easier to decipher rock art in the desert. Plus, her contract with Palladium would be ending next month, and she'd be packing her bags for a new job.

She sighed, glancing back at Kapp, who was eagerly awaiting a reply. "Between juggling my duties for part of the year, I have time for little else."

"And what do you do when the season ends?"

"I work all year at different contract jobs," she snapped. "Winter is spent doing online cataloging of the hundreds of mineshafts that dot this region; after that, I spend time giving public-awareness presentations around the West to get more eyes on the safety issues involved with these old tunnels before some kid or dayhiker falls to their death or gets trapped during the rainy season."

She could tell by his demeanor that he was going to continue peppering her with probing personal questions, and she needed to wrap up his visit. "So, why don't you direct any further questions to Sheriff Dewey, who grew up here and knows this area better than anyone."

His expression soured. "Very well, but perhaps we could discuss your work over..."

She thrust her hand out to the horizon. "You should probably be shoving off. See that brown squall line out there...that's the makings of a sandstorm. You can probably clear this region if you leave now, but I wouldn't delay too long. I'd hate for you to be stuck on the road in your vehicle. Storms like that can last for days."

She didn't wait for him to respond, pivoting and leading him towards his dusty white Camry.

Kapp trotted to keep up with her, glancing pensively over his shoulder. "We never had anything like sandstorms back East where I grew up. How much time before the storm hits?"

"You'll probably have a half hour headstart once you get to the main road."

"But that's miles from here."

"Eight to be exact, and it's the only way in and out of here."

He opened the door, removing his brimmed hat and tossing it inside. "What about you and your crew?"

"We'll pack up and head back to town soon. Just get going so I can help my guys break our camp."

He extended his bony, pale hand. "You're a pioneer woman for working under these conditions."

"Thanks. I appreciate you coming all the way out here and enduring such hardships. You're quite a frontiersman, alright."

He grinned, licking his cracked lips. "Guess so."

She slammed the door, stepping back and watching him race down the road, frequently bottoming out the Camry on the bumpy contours until he was out of sight.

Hearing footsteps behind her, she turned to see Joe Satala and the other tech heading towards the open tailgate of their truck.

"We're gonna get our tents set up before the wind gets any worse," said Joe.

She nodded in approval. "Think I'll do the same. The weather forecast I saw this morning said things weren't going to get nasty until tomorrow, but this doesn't look like a night to spend out in the open on my cot."

"Yeah, you can never tell if that *sandstorm* is going to head our way." He chuckled, glancing down the road that Kapp was on.

"Hey, I needed to get rid of that cretin." She walked to her company Suburban, opening the driver's door and removing a bottle of sunscreen to replenish the coating on her skin. Between the wind and sun, the desert could turn a person into driftwood.

When she was done, she grabbed the two-way radio off the dashboard, turning it off to conserve the battery since reception on the mesa was spotty given that their campsite was bordered by a U-shaped cluster of low ridges.

They still had a few hours of work left, but she was already looking forward to collapsing on top of her sleeping bag and enjoying the serenade of leaves on the rustling sycamore trees beyond her vehicle.

CHAPTER 10

AFTER TROTTING along a flat stretch of ground for a quarter mile, Mercer came to the base of a faint incline that headed up towards the top of Black Canyon and began the slow upward trek that led to the rim of the eight-hundred-foot gorge.

While he would have better concealment in the interior, the serpentine contours of the canyon would add considerable miles onto his trip, and he would be contending with navigating over van-sized boulders for the upper half, which posed too great a risk to his ankles and knees.

Walking up the slope, his profile was exposed, so he picked up the pace until he reached a cluster of juniper trees at the halfway point. The sixty-pound backpack and the eighty-degree heat caused a rivulet of sweat to run down his forehead. He crouched in the shade, partly to take a short break but also to scan his surroundings. He removed his binoculars and glassed the route he'd just taken.

Since departing his cabin, he'd kept up a vigorous pace, covering a little over two miles in the past hour.

The flies and gnats had already discovered his presence

and began their assault on his neck and face. It was always like this after the summer rains when the rockholes and basins in the canyons were brimming with insect life.

He swatted away the vampire bugs, his ears attuned to the rotary birdsong of a nearby wren. When he was assured no one was on his immediate trail, he scanned to the south, observing the eastern edge of Black Canyon, which was laced with clumps of ankle-high prickly-pear cactus and narrowleaf yucca interspersed with the occasional pinon pine tree clinging tenaciously to the rim. These would be his companions during the trek to the San Juan River.

He lowered the binoculars, returning his gaze towards the distant mouth of the canyon, just over two miles beyond to where his cabin was located.

By now, he figured the pursuers in the two vehicles he saw earlier on the dead man's tablet would have discovered his truck parked at Badger Gulch. They would probably keep a few men there to see if anything turned up while the rest of the team headed to his cabin and used that as an incident command post.

Mercer licked his lips, wondering if Dewey had been roped into the manhunt and what story Crowe had fed to the sheriff. Was Mercer being painted as a rogue CIA agent or a villain in some fictitious story that suited Crowe's agenda? He knew that Crowe only had to look in the mirror for an example of a ruthless and avaricious character to fit the latter, and he was certain that Crowe would try to manipulate the sheriff at every opportunity.

He respected Dewey and always felt like the man was meant for bigger things than Blayne. From what he'd pieced together from locals over the years, Dewey's career took a drastic turn after he first joined the sheriff's department months after returning from the academy.

The sheriff back then was Jake Sedgewidth, who had run things in Southeast Utah with an Old West sense of justice for the past forty years. Mercer didn't necessarily object to that except for Sedgewidth's reputation for fabricating evidence to suit his needs.

A month after Dewey joined the three-man department, the bullet-riddled body of John Hanover was discovered in an arroyo on the north end of town. The man had been shot in the back, and the only other tracks in the sandy wash were some small prints typical in size for a woman.

Everyone in town knew of John Hanover's drunken rages and the beatings that his wife Nancy endured on a weekly basis.

As far as Sheriff Sedgewidth was concerned, justice had been served, and he removed the photos of Nancy's tracks from the evidence file, closing the case.

Only the matter of altering the findings and adjusting the law to fit the narrative didn't sit well with Dewey, who believed that the legal system should have decided Nancy's fate.

At great risk to his own career, he anonymously slipped Sedgewidth's actions to the attorney general in Salt Lake, who launched an investigation into Sedgewidth's past, uncovering dozens of other cases where he'd tampered with evidence or dished out his own brand of vigilante justice.

Sedgewidth and one other deputy were arrested while the others resigned and moved out of state. At twenty-four, Arlo Dewey became the face of law-enforcement in San Juan County and a recognized officer in the communities around Four Corners as the *sheriff who couldn't be corrupted*.

For a few years, he became a celebrated speaker at law-enforcement conventions and was touted by the attorney general as the next generation of officers while Old West vigilantism and cowboy justice was finally laid to rest.

But the ripple effect of his actions would affect more than Dewey's career: Nancy Hanover and her thirteen-year-old daughter paid the ultimate price. The mother went to jail for manslaughter, and her daughter suffered in the hands of the foster care system, eventually committing suicide a year into her mother's sentence.

Mercer never let on that he knew about the full extent of Dewey's early years as sheriff, but he figured that the gray hairs on the forty-year-old's head weren't from his current duties in Blayne.

Now, as he gazed at the canyon ahead, Mercer hoped that Dewey would escape the brunt of trouble that he had just brought to his friend's doorstep.

CHAPTER 11

DEACON CROWE GLANCED around the frugal interior of the cabin. He coughed at the overpowering odor of chemicals, pulling his sleeve up to his nose as his eyes watered.

Making his way to the kitchen, he found the source of his irritation in the kitchen sink. He slid back the window then used a spatula on the counter to flip the laptop onto its side and remove the drain plug. The device wouldn't be of any use now, but he didn't need to melt his olfactory glands while he was using Mercer's place as his command post.

"Open up the rest of the windows in this place," he barked at Dewey, who was lingering near the back door.

Crowe meandered through the living room, his eyes floating over the knotty pine walls and meager furnishings. He made his way to the side office, which was mostly used as a small library filled with floor-to-ceiling shelves made of cherry containing books on Southwestern birds, animal tracks, edible plants, geology, native culture, prehistory and an odd assortment of old texts on Roman history and Greek mythology.

He pulled a tattered copy of *Dune* from the shelf.

The guys lives in the fucking desert and he's reading this book? he thought.

Crowe recalled another time halfway around the world when he and the man he'd now come to know as Nick Mercer worked in counter-insurgency throughout Africa, existing only as personnel numbers within the Special Activities Division at Langley.

He tossed the book on the table in the corner, noticing the generic photos on the wall of waterfalls and sunset vistas over the mountains. Besides the bookshelf, nothing in the place revealed anything about the man, and Crowe thought about how the residents of Blayne had no idea of the wolf that had been lying dormant in their midst.

"So, you say Mercer was a woodworker during all the time you knew him?" he shouted back to Dewey in the other room.

"That's right. Mainly made high-end furniture out of local wood and sold the pieces to clients up north."

That'd make sense and would be a decent cover story, given that your old man was a carpenter. Good for you, "Nick."

Crowe heard his earpiece crackle, tapping on it.

"We've driven along some of the dirt roads north of town and haven't seen any signs of a lone hiker," said the voice of Jiya, one of his African mercenaries. "Do you want us to check to the south or west?"

"No. Let's regroup at my location. I'll send you the coordinates."

He signed off then returned to the living room, standing across from Dewey. "Anyone Mercer was close to here... hunting buddies, neighbors, maybe a girlfriend?" Crowe studied Dewey's expression closely at the mention of the last word.

"He got along with everyone and was well liked. He was

involved for a bit with a seasonal employee named Angela Owens. She's surveying old mining sites in the county for a private firm out of Denver. But their relationship, if it can even be called that, didn't last long."

"Why not?"

"You'd have to ask one of them. None of my business."

He knew the man was covering for one or both of them. In a town like this, everyone's business was known, especially by the sheriff. He needed to find out if Dewey was close enough to Mercer to aid in his escape or to interfere with the coming manhunt.

For now, he needed to keep the sheriff close.

Dewey removed his cowboy hat, scratching his head. "So, in the past, we normally worked with the FBI field office out of Durango...Dave Nash and Paul Whittaker."

"Yeah, good guys. They were tied up in Denver, and we were just heading back to Durango after doing some annual training with the U.S. Marshals outside of Moab." He held up his cellphone. "Speaking of the Durango office, I need to place a call, so you'll have to excuse me for a few minutes."

He stepped outside the cabin, walking past the vehicles as he dialed his employer. "I have narrowed down where Hendrix is at...he now goes by the name Nick Mercer."

"That's the best news I've heard all week," said Edgar Rohrbach in a gravelly South African accent with its Dutch influence. "How long before you have him?"

"He should be in our hands shortly. He's on the run, but not much of anything out here for him to escape to."

"Get what you came for even if it means softening him up, then get the hell out of there."

"I don't plan to linger any longer than necessary. As it is, I can keep this town locked down for another twenty-four hours before the locals start asking too many questions and our roadblocks start drawing suspicions from the authorities up north. With that in mind, I need your hackers to put a blanket over the cellphone towers in this region until we leave."

"Consider it done."

"And one last thing...what do you want me to do with Hendrix once we've got the diamonds?"

"I'll leave that to your discretion."

"Copy that, sir. When you hear from me again, we'll be on the jet heading back with your prized possession and Hendrix's scalp."

CHAPTER 12

PRETORIA, **South Africa**

EDGAR ROHRBACH SLID his phone back into the pocket of his tan dress pants then stepped out onto the veranda of his three-story estate, staring at the distant mountain range then tracing his holdings back down to the lush gardens bordering his nine-hundred-acre vineyard.

"Good news from abroad, I trust?" said Thomas Bowen, the CEO of Rohrbach's company, who was seated at an oaken table, smoking a cigar.

"We'll see. It shouldn't be long now until I have those diamonds." His face was as rigid as his voice was tense.

"How long after we get them before our scientists can determine the mineral core where they originated in those Liberian valleys?"

Edgar gave the man a shrewd look. "You never did bother to learn the science."

"I leave that to you, my friend. My job is to be the public face of the company and maintain international relations with our buyers so you can go on doing what you do behind the scenes."

"If they are still uncut, then they'll be able to identify the microscopic traces of kimberlite on the surface, which we will then be able to match up with samples taken from the hundreds of surface mining sites in Liberia. After that, I'll be able to home in on the location where those red beauties can be found in greater concentration."

Edgar leaned both of his manicured hands on the teak railing, glancing at his servants tending the vineyard below. "You know, when my grandfather Edward first arrived in Africa from the Netherlands nearly eighty years ago, regions like this were a no-man's land, occupied only by the occasional goat herder or seasonal gold prospector. The man lived in a musty canvas tent for two years while scratching in the dirt like all the other miners who'd rushed out here to make their fortune. But one thing he realized was that real wealth would never come just from digging in the mud but from the man who held the reins over the land itself."

"He was a visionary, buying out everyone around him over the years," said Bowen. "And from another age of pioneers who were tough as hell."

"And fucking ruthless."

Edgar silently reflected on his grandfather's colorful stories about his frontier days in the valleys in Liberia and Sierra Leone. The man's full-sized portrait adorned each of the Rohrbach family homes in Pretoria, Tuscany and the Bahamas, and Edgar made sure that biographical sketches of Edward were scrubbed of his mafia business tactics of extorting, bribing and murdering his competitors.

While most miners during his grandfather's time only thought of next year's profits, Edward always said that a man must think beyond his patch of dirt, and he spent most of his life acquiring and consolidating his land holdings to create an empire that eventually controlled the flow of diamonds into the retail showrooms of buyers in London, Hong Kong and New York.

But what his grandfather, and later father, had spent decades trying to achieve, nature had provided in only a few years to Edgar with the arrival of an Ebola outbreak, setting the stage for him to sweep in and forcefully take the remaining mines.

Now, all he needed was the red diamonds so he could trace their origins. Once he had control of that deposit, he would be able to prevent any competitors from flooding the market with those rare gemstones, which would only have a devastating ripple effect on prices...prices that he and his family had had a stranglehold on for nearly a century.

Bowen stamped out the remains of his cigar then stood up. "I need to return to Joburg for a meeting with the rest of the board. By the way, we're having our annual corporate getaway next month. I hope you will be making an appearance?"

He turned, pursing his lips. "Of course. I'll drop by for a few hours. Where will it be this time?"

"Virgin Islands."

"Perfect."

Bowen patted the man on his shoulder. "Try and relax. That problem-solver of yours will get things under control in America. Nothing more you can do right now." He waved his hand out to the mountains. "You should go out hunting for a bit. It'll take the edge off."

Edgar nodded as the man walked off, knowing that the hunt in Utah was the only one on his mind, and after today, its results would reshape his empire for another generation to come.

CHAPTER 13

Plum-orange slivers of sunlight stabbed through the cottonwood branches above Mercer's head from the fading rays of dusk.

He had remained in his concealed position for the past thirty minutes, scanning the opposite rim of Black Canyon, the gorge below, and the faint animal trail he'd trotted after leaving his cabin. This time, his binoculars were replaced with the scope on his takedown MK12 rifle.

Since departing his home, he'd managed to cover just over three miles, a little over two along the peninsula that led from his abode to the mouth of Black Canyon then another mile beside the western rim of the canyon.

Though he'd done this route many times with Luce, it was always with a small daypack during the cooler months of spring and fall. He'd pushed his body before under more grueling conditions, but now, his knees and back were reminding him of the years of training missions and airborne jumps, making him feel like he was well beyond the approaching horizon of forty.

Mercer waited for another hour until the darkness

required him to flick on the night-vision scope on his rifle, giving him a better look at the undulating terrain.

Fifteen minutes into his scan of the areas to the north near the beginning of Black Canyon, he saw the man. Though Mercer had covered several miles on foot since skirting the rim near the top of the canyon, it was a sinuous route, and from his current position, he was now observing a distance of just under a mile to the mouth as the crow flies.

The man was tall, clad in BDU pants, boots, windbreaker and boonie hat. He carried a rifle at a low-ready. The figure paused every few feet, studying the tracks before continuing on.

Not likely you're a dayhiker.

He adjusted the elevation and windage dials on his scope, accounting for the light southerly breeze wafting along the rim and the approximate fifteen-hundred-yard distance. He had no desire to risk attempting a shot from this angle and distance but wanted to track the man's movements to see how many were in the pursuit group and whether they would pick up his route along the rim.

Plus, he didn't want to reveal his position by sniping one guy, figuring the enemy had portable drones or possibly even satellite overwatch on the area.

He watched the tall man pause and kneel, staring at the ground again then touching his right ear.

Is he communicating with others around him or just back to base...my cabin, probably?

A few seconds later, the man stopped once more at the base of the sandstone slope Mercer had ascended earlier, then he disappeared out of sight.

Mercer kept his gaze fixed on the top of the rim, where the edge of the mesa seemed to melt into the canyon. Occasionally, he would scan down below, but after fifteen minutes, he surmised that the man had probably continued along the mesa rather than heading south towards Mercer.

Or he's going to circle in from another direction rather than risk walking straight towards me.

He thought about the pursuer and the confidence and ease with which he moved along with the fact that the man was only a few miles behind him.

He's hunted at night before...and he knows how to read the ground. Mercer wasn't surprised, but his concern came from knowing that it took considerable skills and nerve to hunt alone in the dark and in unfamiliar territory.

All the more reason to keep moving.

He was about to slide back from his overwatch and retrieve his pack when he heard a faint sound to his rear.

Mercer felt his heart punching through his ribs, remaining still and slowly turning on his side as he pointed the suppressed rifle towards the shrubs beyond his boots.

How could they have pinpointed me this fast? Could they have inserted from the south?

He chided himself for being so forward-focused that he'd let his attention to the rear slip. Now, he was backed up against the rim with only cactus and boulders along either side.

The noise stopped.

He swept his rifle slowly from right to left, scanning the dense foliage beyond for any movement. Just as he was about to sit up, there was a rush of sound on the dry leaves to his left. The tight confines beside the juniper prevented him from using his rifle, and he quickly slid it onto his lap as he withdrew his Glock 17.

He swiveled on his right hip, but it was too late; the figure darted beyond the branches towards his face.

Mercer aimed towards the noise then lowered his index finger onto the trigger. Just before he was about to shoot, he saw the four-legged beast spring from the shadows, the black-and-tan coat visible in the moonlight, sending reassurance that he wasn't going to be devoured. Luce leapt onto his chest, licking his face and swinging her hips as her tail wagged without restraint.

Mercer set down the pistol, holding her sides and pulling her close, the dusty odor of her coat filling the air. "You scared the shit out of me, girl. What the hell are you doing here?"

She pressed her muzzle under his chin, melting into his chest, and Mercer felt like she had never left his side. He figured the crafty dog must have bolted out of the door when Jessica returned home, or perhaps she had pried free one of the partly open windows.

Either way, she was here now, which meant his objectives of time and distance were in need of serious readjustment.

He leaned his head back onto the ground, staring up at the stars as he stroked the dog's neck.

CHAPTER 14

For the past two hours, Dewey had watched the FBI team tear apart Mercer's cabin and surrounding outbuildings. Clearly they were looking for something specific, but the sheriff could only make out snippets of information between the men. He found it odd that his assistance hadn't been requested and his deputies had been instructed to stand watch at the two prominent trailheads even though no signs of Mercer were evident.

Crowe had a definite command presence to him, but he reminded Dewey of an old silverback gorilla he'd seen at the zoo in Salt Lake, the creature exerting its authority by waving a hefty log around towards anyone who glanced at him.

And the FBI agents were an odd assemblage of men with varying accents that Dewey couldn't place.

"Do you need my deputies to man the roadblocks you guys set up at either end of town? They're not really doing much sitting in their trucks at the trailheads," he said when Crowe came in through the back door.

"We've got it handled. Your guys can just remain in position for now in case Mercer shows himself."

"O-K." Dewey got up from the stool beside the fireplace and headed to the kitchen to get a bottle of water from his daypack on the floor. While he sipped, he leaned his hip against the edge of the sandstone countertop, watching the other agents inspecting the attic and closets again.

The FBI agent named Atley, whom Crowe indicated was his second-in-command, hadn't looked up from his laptop once except to take a swig from an energy drink. Dewey was growing impatient with the lack of communication on the search for Mercer, not to mention how there was a lack of the usual protocols he'd come to expect from federal agents pursuing a fugitive.

As far as he knew, there had been none of the usual back and forth with FBI headquarters in Denver or Salt Lake, no effort to enlist the help of him or his deputies in navigating through backcountry that they knew intimately, and no requests to bring any additional law-enforcement officers from Monticello or Moab to assist with roadblocks.

Dewey still couldn't believe Mercer could be tied up in the atrocities in Africa that Crowe described, but he felt compelled to play his part as local law-enforcement. If nothing else, it would help him ascertain more details about Crowe's agenda and may even help bring in Mercer alive instead of as a bullet-riddled corpse. The former would provide answers to much-needed questions that were clawing away at Dewey about the man he had thought was a trusted friend.

I couldn't have been that far off the mark about him all these years.

He shuffled forward a few feet, glancing at Atley's laptop

screen, which showed what looked like a thermal image of the desert area southwest of the cabin.

"Is that satellite feed?" he said.

Atley pivoted his chair, angling his computer away. "Just overlaying a new software program onto the topographic map here to better determine what route this guy Mercer might be taking."

"If he's heading south then there's only two ways to proceed. He either has to skirt along the rim of Black Canyon for about twelve miles before dropping down at a fault line near the middle section or he can travel overland a half-mile to the west and get into Gould Canyon, which is a little less rocky."

Atley frowned. "And take it to where? There's nothing out in this wasteland."

"Well, that's the question, isn't it?" Dewey folded his arms. "Either route takes him through some nasty terrain with miles of cactus, car-sized boulders that can snap an ankle, and rattlers. Then again, Nick knows the area better than almost any of the locals here, including me, and I grew up here."

Crowe came up beside the sheriff, rolling his head back and forth as he stretched. "'Nick'? You guys drinking buddies?"

"Just friends, like I said earlier." He pointed his thumb over his shoulder to the scattering of photos on the counter. "Those photos you showed me before of what Nick was supposedly responsible for doing over in Africa years ago… if that's all true, why would he risk showing up back here in the U.S.? I mean, why not disappear over in Eastern Europe or Panama?"

Atley interjected, raising his hands up. "We just get assigned the cases and track down the whackos."

Dewey noted the man's slight southern accent. "You from South Carolina or Georgia, by chance?"

"Uhm, Savannah, Georgia."

"Ah, I wondered. I attended the law-enforcement training center in Glynco on the north side of Savannah. Amazing place."

Atley nodded. "Yep, they crank out a lot of officers there."

Except Glynco is an hour south of Savannah in the town of Brunswick.

Dewey felt his stomach coil in knots, feeling like the cabin walls were constricting. He tried to convince himself the agent was distracted by the chase, but there were just too many inconsistencies in Crowe's and Atley's responses.

What are these guys up to? Is Mercer really who they say he is? And what are they searching for in this cabin?

Atley abruptly slid his chair forward, his gaze zeroing in on his laptop. "Got you, motherfucker."

He picked up his headset. "Three, this is Two, over."

Dewey couldn't make out Atley's replies but moved slightly to get a better glimpse of the computer screen, which showed a high-resolution image of the topography surrounding Blayne with two prominent red blips, confirming his suspicions about satellite capabilities.

Didn't realize the Feds were so high-tech these days. He glanced again at the blips, figuring the second, slower-moving one was Luce, but he felt reluctant to volunteer the information. *Why would a stone-cold killer like they've made Nick out to be take his dog along with him?*

Crowe nodded for Dewey to follow him into the office, where a large topographic map of the area was laid out on the table.

"So, if you were Mercer, which way would you go?"

Dewey figured the man was trying to distract from what Atley was doing, but he had little choice but to play along.

"Well, if he heads north, he'll be getting into some higher elevations in the Blue Mountains and some potentially colder temps, plus he's more likely to have run-ins with deer hunters in that area."

Deacon pointed to the west. "He'll have to cross this one highway eventually, but what's the terrain like?"

"PJ—pinon juniper—so lots of scrub and not much for concealment. Not too hilly, just miles of monotonous country without any water."

Dewey traced his finger to the south. "That way, he'll eventually dead-end at the San Juan River forty-five miles before it dumps into Lake Powell. That's a helluva long haul on foot...probably fifteen miles if you add in all the bends in the canyons. Plus, once he got to the river, he'd need a canoe or somethin' to get across."

"Across to where?" Crowe tapped on the vast expanse of desert south of the San Juan River. "This is just a big blank spot."

"Navajo Reservation...largest Rez in the country. Takes about four hours just to drive east to west, and there are still some folks who live out there only speaking Navajo and doing sheepherdin' for a living." He tapped on a string of roads west of Monument Valley. "Heck, in a few areas, they just had dirt roads put in there twenty years back, and a handful of old-timers live in log hogans, hauling their water in buckets from springs."

Crowe shook his head, wondering if he was still in North America. "So, which way would you go if you were in Mercer's boots?"

Dewey folded his arms, staring down at the map for a long time. "He's someone who knows the land and what it can provide. And from what you've described of his training, he probably knows how to live off that land for as long as necessary." He leaned his hands on the table, scanning the topography again, then gazed up at Crowe. "Who's to say he's going to make a beeline in any of those directions? What if he's going to just stay out there until your search efforts are exhausted?"

"Not likely if I call in the Bureau, requesting more personnel and air assets so we can stage a full-scale manhunt over this entire region."

"Happened already once out here about twenty-five years ago. Three survival nuts went on a rampage, shootin' up a patrol car and killing a deputy then took off on the run through the canyons southeast of here. There were hundreds of LEOs from several different alphabet agencies...even some Navajo trackers. Two of the guys were eventually found, but they had died of their own self-inflicted gunshot wounds. The third guy's body was only discovered by a cowboy about ten years ago."

Dewey arched up. "This is country that chews people up and never spits them out. Heck, archeologists still find actual mummified remains of prehistoric people from fifteen hundred years ago in caves in the backcountry around here, so I'd say Mercer could play a waiting game if he wanted to."

CROWE KNEW the sheriff was just postulating implausible scenarios to avoid giving a definitive answer. By the way he described the southern route to the San Juan River, it seemed like he had intimate knowledge of the challenges along the way, and since Mercer was on Dewey's search-

and-rescue team, the man had probably grown quite familiar with using that as a potential evasion route. Plus, it was the only direction that didn't involve a risky road crossing where he might be sighted.

That's the way I'd go, then I'd have a buddy pick me up in a raft at that river.

He shot a sideways glance at Dewey. "Maybe you're right about his ability to hold out, eatin' snakes and shit, but eventually all fugitives have to rear their head." He nodded towards the other room. "Besides, Atley picked up a second blip—small one, which means he's got his dog with him. At least I assume it's his dog since he's got a couple of bowls on the kitchen floor."

"Luce...she's a cattle dog he rescued from the Rez after someone tossed her into a ditch."

Crowe emitted a plastic smile, lightly clapping his hands. "Aw, he sounds like such a swell guy."

"The person I knew was a good dude. I still can't believe he's a war criminal."

"I'll relay your sentiments to the judge during his trial, right after the part about him gunning down one of my men."

Crowe pursed his lips. The sheriff had outgrown his usefulness. "You have been extremely helpful, but I think we can take it from here. Maybe you oughta check on your deputies?"

Dewey gave a reluctant nod then headed out the front door. He walked down the steps, pausing briefly to make out enough of Atley's conversation to learn that Mercer and Luce were on foot somewhere about a mile north of the fault line on the western side of Black Canyon.

The sound of crunching gravel drew his attention to the road, and he pivoted around to see headlights from one of his deputies' cruisers. The man pulled in beside the FBI vehicles as Dewey walked over to the driver's side, leaning in the open window.

"Wes, thought you were supposed to be staking out the parking area for Badger Gulch?"

The young man with short black hair was no older than Dewey when he began as a deputy. Though Wesley Bruchac had been a recent hire, he had proven very diligent and had taken to the work, even volunteering his services during his days off.

"I had to drive a couple of dayhikers back to town. They got turned around and ended up finishing on the wrong side of the mesa. Tried calling you, but the radios aren't working. Neither is my cellphone."

Dewey glanced down the road. "Must be some kinda outage going on."

"I talked to a couple people on the way over here, and they also said they couldn't get reception. Doesn't seem to matter which provider neither."

"We just got two new towers near Montezuma Creek and up by Blanding a few months ago, so that doesn't seem right." Dewey glanced past the two vehicles, seeing the silhouette of Atley through the cabin curtains; the man was still fixated on his laptop. "It's been a helluva weird day."

Dewey leaned in closer to his deputy. "Wes, I want you to take a drive over to Matt Harrigan's place. See if his HAM radio is still able to get a signal."

"It should be...that antenna takes up half his backyard."

He pointed to the man's ledger on the passenger's seat. "Hand me that. I'm gonna jot down two names. Contact the dispatcher at the FBI office in Durango—Matt will know how to look that up—then see what they say about the two field agents on this list. You'll have to give them your badge number, and mine as well, but it shouldn't take long to get an answer. Just keep this between us, and tell Matt to stay quiet too. And if the phones or radios suddenly start working, don't trying calling me, just meet me at the Badger Gulch parking lot when you're done."

"OK, boss. You got it." The young deputy gazed at the men milling around in the cabin. "What's going on...why they after Nick?"

"Not sure yet, but Nick might not be the guy we all thought he was."

———

CROWE SNAPPED HIS FINGERS, gathering the rest of his team around Atley's laptop. "Keep tearing this place apart then get into his toolshed and do the same. At sunrise, we'll head south and try to pick up a road leading into this canyon where the target is located. Atley will remain here to run comms. I wanna wrap up this guy Mercer by noon so we can get out of this dustbowl and back to Joburg."

"What about Jiya?" said Atley. "He picked up the guy's tracks moving south along Black Canyon but said it's slow going."

Crowe glanced down at the computer screen, watching the two red blips slowly heading south. "Tell him to stay in pursuit but to keep his distance, and I'll be in touch with him as soon as we're coming in from the south at daybreak. Then we'll close in from both directions."

———

AFTER RECEIVING HIS ORDERS, Jiya proceeded towards a U-shaped cluster of small boulders that would provide ample cover for the night and give him a view of the canyon to the south. From the tracks on the ground, he'd learned that his quarry had been doing short bursts of quick walking then slowing to a normal pace during the inclines in elevation. From the short stride and depth of the heel impressions, it was evident that he was carrying a decent load on his back.

With each twist in the trail, Jiya had been expecting a potential ambush, but it soon became clear that the man was intent on putting as much distance as he could between him and the town.

Jiya removed his daypack then plunked down, removing a plastic canteen and sipping the tepid water. In between drinks, his nose searched the air, only detecting the spicy aroma from some unknown trees to the left and the rotting odor of decaying cowpies.

This place was far different than the jungles of Sierra Leone, and he was grateful that the area wasn't inhabited by the cobras, malaria and ghastly parasites that had plagued his youth as a child soldier.

Despite the constant threat of environmental dangers in his homeland, if there was one thing he had learned in his twenty-three years, it was that the greatest danger in the wilds always came from his own species. There was no other creature on the planet that delighted in inflicting horror like men did. And the hungrier the man, whether for land, riches or just plain hunger, the more savage the outcome.

In this case, he was relieved it was just one person that Crowe was after, which meant less bloodshed for a change. But it was the diamonds in Hendrix's possession that had quickened Jiya's pace all day. He was determined to find a way of getting to the man before Crowe did, which was why he would press on with his trek south before dawn despite his boss's recent orders.

Just a few diamonds that Crowe won't ever know about. He thought of the looks of adoration that he'd get, driving through his village in a new truck before winding up the road to his red-brick home on the hillside that towered above the tin shacks below.

His pulse raced, knowing that the only thing between him and his dreams right now was a few miles of rock and cactus.

CHAPTER 15

MERCER AND LUCE walked for another mile on the animal trail skirting the canyon rim, stopping around midnight due to the rocky terrain becoming too treacherous.

He set his pack down beside a sandstone rock spire that resembled a giant jutting from the earth. He had chosen the area because it was choked with cactus, making an approach difficult, and he and the dog had taken their time weaving cautiously through the maze of succulents.

The immense rock spire was angled enough to provide a slight overhang on one side, and he kicked aside some old cowpies, scanning the ground for scorpions, which often used the decaying matter for shelter.

When he was sure there weren't any immediate threats from rattlesnakes, centipedes or other creepy-crawlies, he removed a poncho liner from his pack, stretching it out on the sandy substrate. Under where his hip would rest, he scooped out an inch of sand so he could at least have a small measure of comfort while he rested.

He thought of just leaning back against the rock spire for a few hours but knew that would only result in a stiff back and poor sleep. Right now, he needed a few hours of rest to be ready for the grueling trek at first light.

With the air temps hovering in the mid-60s and a ground temperature a few degrees higher, there was little concern about hypothermia.

With his crude bed ready, he lay down, placing the MK12 beside him and resting on his left hip, which allowed easy access to the Glock on his right side.

As she'd done countless times before, Luce settled in by his knees after digging a small depression in the ground beside him, her head up as she kept watch on their surroundings. Mercer was the only member of her flock that she had to safeguard, and he always rested easier knowing her sharp senses were inspecting the land for threats.

The wind was still blowing from the south, which was an unusual change he'd noted earlier. Normally, the diurnal winds of the desert flowed from the south during the day, shifting to the north at night as the cooler air settled down canyon.

The abrupt change in direction meant there was either a shift in low pressure bringing in a storm from the direction of Arizona or there was just upper-atmosphere turbulence typical of the mountain West, which meant high winds tomorrow.

He welcomed the latter, knowing it could help obliterate signs of his passage, but it also meant his hearing would be reduced and Luce's ability to detect scents would be hampered. Even she didn't like being out on windy days since her primary sense was skewed.

Mercer laid his head against the pack, calming his breathing and trying to get his tense shoulders to relax, hoping the rock spire would provide enough cover to thwart any satellite reconnaissance above.

He glanced at his watch, knowing he had four hours until dawn, then mentally set an alarm to be up an hour before. He rested his hand on Luce's neck, closing his eyes and relying on his unconscious to alert him to any sudden changes in their surroundings.

CHAPTER 16

LANGLEY, **Virginia**

0715 EST

NEIL PATTERSON TOSSED his raincoat and briefcase on the couch against the window, the scowl on his face growing deeper with each passing minute since he'd arrived at his office on the seventh floor. He'd had his secretary cancel all of his morning engagements and had summoned an Agency pilot to prep his jet for a 0815 departure.

Now, all he needed was answers to a slew of questions from a man he knew would be unlikely or unwilling to part with them.

As the Director of Clandestine Field Operations, he oversaw hundreds of agents and numerous missions around the globe. With three decades in the intelligence community, he had worked at almost every level within field ops, from the Special Activities Division to co-founding an elite

Search and Destroy Unit with colleague Ryan Foley, who still headed up the small cadre of assassin-hunters. But a growing collection of injuries eventually caught up with Patterson, which was what led to him being appointed to his current role.

Now, he was worried that months of clandestine work on a particular operation were about to unravel in the coming hours. And the fact that this one was being conducted outside of the jurisdiction of the CIA on American soil was making his stomach churn like a cement mixer.

He heard a familiar voice outside his office door as his secretary entered followed by Garrett Ryland, Lead Case Officer for the Agency's African Division.

Ryland had cut his teeth with the State Department in North Africa, working in diplomatic security for several years. Given his fluency in French and Arabic, he was later recruited by the CIA, eventually rising up to become a case officer in West Africa. Patterson knew it was a political appointment given the man's many connections in D.C. and Ryland's father having been a lawyer at Langley.

To Patterson, Ryland was a talented interpreter and analyst, but the man had a horrendous track record with managing field operations. His lackluster performance during a botched mission in Sierra Leone five years ago put his abilities in question, but Ryland had powerful friends in D.C., so rather than face early resignation, he was sequestered back to Langley and assigned to an oversight position for the remainder of his days.

Patterson didn't bother standing to greet the man, glancing at his waistline, which seemed to have increased since their last visit.

"You requested my presence, sir?"

The director motioned for the man to sit. "I trust you just got a good night's sleep since it will probably be your last for some time to come." Patterson slid a folder towards the portly man. "This was just flagged by my intel staff."

Ryland's eyes widened as he slowly moved the first black-and-white photograph towards him like it was an ancient scroll. "Where did you get this?" he said without taking his eyes off the man in the image.

"Moab, Utah of all fucking places." Patterson was tapping his fingers on the armrests. "It's from a security camera along Main Street. Taken yesterday morning."

"Why would he rear his head after all this time?"

"I was hoping you could lend some insight."

"He's your boy. You trained him...you tell me."

Patterson gave Ryland a look of disgust. "*Was*...his case file was closed nearly five years ago when he went missing in West Africa after you and your team were supposed to eliminate him. Remember?"

Ryland pressed his fingers against his temples. "Any indication on where he was heading?"

"Satellite imagery from the past twenty-four hours shows him driving south to some Podunk town called Blayne in the middle of the desert, just north of the Arizona border."

"Blayne...never heard of it."

"Nobody has; only a few hundred people live there. Mostly caters to tourists and nature freaks."

Ryland held the photo, staring into the icy eyes of Deacon Crowe. "God help them all if he's there."

"I've got a team on standby in Salt Lake. They can be in Blayne in a few hours via helo."

The last time Patterson had instructed Ryland to kill Deacon Crowe was after the director discovered that the agent had abandoned his duties in Liberia and sold out to a mercenary army in Sierra Leone. It was believed he was working for a wealthy diamond broker out of Johannesburg, but the Agency could never establish a direct link between Crowe and the Rohrbach Mining Company.

The incident had become a festering wound for the Agency, who had invested considerable time and money into Liberia only to have it crumble apart during a devastating Ebola outbreak that tore West Africa apart, plunging many of the coastal nations into civil war. Crowe's involvement in the genocide of thousands of native Liberians was something the Agency wanted to bury. It had become a black cloud hanging over Patterson, since he had trained Crowe and his colleague, Nathan Hendrix, during his previous assignment as a field officer with the Special Activities Division.

Ryland set the photo down and slid it away as if it were suddenly contaminated then went to get up. "I hope they can take him down without incident."

"Hope! There is no hope in this line of business, just meticulous planning and execution, which seems to have eluded your efforts with Crowe in Africa the last time you had boots on the ground. So, *you* need to be in the field on this op, Garrett, to ensure the success of the mission, instead of your usual armchair quarterbacking."

Ryland's eyes narrowed. "The team in Salt Lake are most likely pros and can handle it. I will lend overwatch from here and..."

"I've seen how you *handle* things, which is why I'll also be coming, to make sure this gets tied up for good...before Crowe turns that town into a graveyard."

CHAPTER 17

BY DAWN, Angela Owens had finished her short jog down the dirt road that ran parallel with the lower end of Black Canyon. The forest service road was the only way in from the south, and it abruptly ended a few miles up near the border with the BLM wilderness region that protected millions of acres of untrammeled wilderness accessible only by foot or horseback.

She returned to her company Suburban just in time to see her two techs emerging from their tent. Angela figured they were as tired as her given the unrelenting flapping of their nylon shelters in the wind, which had increased considerably after midnight.

As Angela went about firing up a pot of coffee on the Coleman stove on the tailgate, Joe Satala emerged from his truck, trotting over and handing the two-way radio to her. "It's Dewey. Said he needs to talk with you."

"It can't wait 'til I'm back in town later?"

Satala shook his head. "Sounded urgent. Somethin' about your friend Nick bein' in trouble with the Feds."

The Feds could mean a lot of things, Angela told herself.

Could be he accidentally crossed over onto some BLM land that was off limits while he was scouting for the fall deer hunt, or he was harvesting juniper without a woodcutting permit.

Though she figured Mercer was never that careless. She wondered why Dewey was calling her about the matter so early in the morning.

Does Nick need me to vouch for him to some overzealous law-enforcement officer who ventured down from Salt Lake during their monthly rotation?

When Dewey's words over the radio mentioned *war criminal* and *wanted fugitive*, she stopped in her tracks, her boots cemented to the ground.

"What the hell are you talking about, Arlo?"

"Look, I'm just telling you what the FBI Task Force leader told me. Said Nick was involved in the slaughter of innocent civilians over in some place called Liberia. Africa, he said. Worked as a mercenary, for God's sakes. Guess he's been on the run for years, using different aliases and stolen money."

Angela's eyes narrowed as if she was staring into the sun. "That isn't Nick. There's no way."

"I said the same thing a dozen times already. Believe me. I thought I knew him, but I saw the photos of the villagers he killed. Murdered dozens of people then stole a bunch of diamonds. The Feds and INTERPOL have been searching for him for several years, although the guys that are in Blayne now seem like they have their own agenda."

Angela pressed her hand against her abdomen, remaining silent as she chewed on her lower lip.

"What do you mean? What agenda?"

"Not sure yet. The agent in charge is not following any

protocols I'm familiar with and has been running things like it's his own show rather than a formal investigation."

"How many agents are there?"

"Eight...well, seven now. I guess Mercer killed one of them south of Moab. That's the story anyway."

"He killed a federal agent?"

"Yeah, hard to chew on, I know, but that's what I'm dealing with on this end."

Angela paced back and forth, her eyes scanning the miles of sagebrush on the peninsula nestled between Gould Canyon and Black Canyon.

Dewey continued, "I know this is a lot to take in, but right now, the Feds are asking me and my deputies to clear out anyone in the immediate backcountry and surrounding campgrounds. If you had your damn radio turned on, you'd already know all this."

He sighed. "They hoped to wrap this up by last night, but Mercer is on the run. He may even be heading in your direction. Mercer's location is unknown, and they've already begun a manhunt with their team. They picked up his tracks out back of his cabin, so he may be heading down Black Canyon."

Angela shook her head. "So, Nick, the same guy who's helped you rescue dozens of lost hikers over the years and raised little Luce from a pup...he's a wanted criminal?"

"Angela, you can wrap your head around this later, but right now, I need you and your techs to pull up stakes and head back to town. Anyone else you run across on the return drive, tell them to do the same. The Feds have asked us not to mention anything specifically about Mercer...just say that there's an escaped fugitive in the Four Corners area."

"That doesn't make any sense. Why would they demand

that if they know he's in the region? Wouldn't they bring in the deputies from up north to help shut down the whole county?"

There was a pregnant pause before Dewey responded. "Look, this isn't my show. I gotta run, but get your crew out of there."

He signed off, leaving her listening to the static and staring at the hazy sun cresting the ridgeline, sensing that there really was a powerful storm about to sweep through the region.

CHAPTER 18

THIRTY MINUTES after Dewey's call to head back to town, Angela and her two techs had finished stowing the last of their survey equipment and personal belongings in the two vehicles along with sealing up the vertical passage using plywood boards secured with nails.

"Take everything back to the storage shed then get us all some rooms in town for the night," she said, flipping up the tailgate of her Suburban.

"What about you?" said Satala.

"I'll be a couple minutes behind. Just gonna grab a few items I left up at Last Chance Mine. If those FBI guys end up out here, they're just going to stampede through the area and destroy my monitoring equipment, and weeks of my work will be washed down the drain."

Satala thrust his chin towards the horizon. "I listened to the weather report earlier, and these winds are supposed to get worse, so don't be too worried about getting all that stuff up there."

The older field tech waved goodbye, then the two men

climbed into the battered old Toyota, heading down the narrow road.

Angela followed behind in their dusty wake for a mile then sped off to the left. The seldom-used road transitioned from sugar-sand in sections to tawny slickrock as she drove up a slight incline towards a hundred-foot escarpment of jagged rocks that hugged the western edge of Black Canyon. The formation looked like the vertebrae of an immense creature lying dormant in the Earth.

Another hundred yards of white-knuckle driving along the rocky road and she reached the end, parking next to the brittle stump of an old pine that had lost its battle with the elements long ago.

Angela grabbed her daypack and brimmed hat then slammed the door, trudging up the slickrock to where the plateau levelled off towards Black Canyon near where two rock fissures came together, leading into the inner gorge.

With the wind momentarily subsiding, she heard a far-off hum behind her, the mechanical sound echoing off the cliffs.

Pausing, Angela glanced towards the distant reflection of her white vehicle then a few miles beyond, seeing a black SUV heading up the road towards her.

CHAPTER 19

A HALF-HOUR BEFORE SUNRISE, Mercer had packed up his bedroll and downed half a pouch of food from his MRE packet, giving the remainder to Luce, who reluctantly lapped up the synthetic food.

Mercer had slept fitfully, waking occasionally at the scurrying of kangaroo rats in the cactus or the wind splashing sand on his face, but he always rested more easily with Luce by his side.

During the next two hours, he skirted along the edge of Black Canyon, stopping on occasion to scan the terrain around him for signs of movement. If Crowe and his men were on his trail, they weren't showing any obvious signs, which told him they were still scouring the area for his presence.

By now Crowe must've consulted Dewey to get the lie of the land, but combing eleven million acres of roadless wilderness was going to be time consuming, and Mercer figured that Crowe would send teams of his men into the canyons closest to Blayne that corresponded with the direction of travel Mercer had taken when he departed his cabin.

That he'd only seen one tracker on his trail last night was puzzling, and he suspected Crowe was planning to drive into the region and then fan out on foot. All the more reason why Mercer had to pick up his pace to make it to the fissure in the canyon and drop below.

A half-mile later, he saw the familiar access point that led to the bottom of Black Canyon, the angled rock chute created by a geologic fault line. Once he dropped below, he'd have ample concealment in the maze of cottonwood trees dotting the bottom. This section of Black Canyon was also less serpentine than the headwaters, and it would be easier going with more places for cover.

After two miles in the canyon, he would hike out on an old sheepherder's trail then trot a mile east towards Gould Canyon. Hopefully, his pursuers would still be searching the Black while he prepared his escape on the San Juan River.

Mercer paused in a cluster of young junipers. Dropping to one knee, he raised up his rifle and scanned the terrain ahead. There was a strange absence of birds, and he figured the harsh wind was causing the wildlife to hole up for whatever was heading their way. It was during a brief respite in the unrelenting wind that he heard the sound.

He swept his rifle to the right, glassing the miles of sagebrush blanketing the peninsula of land between Black Canyon and Gould Canyon. Then he saw it: a black SUV racing along the old jeep trail.

Upon coming to the fork in the road, they veered to the right instead of making a beeline towards him, which meant they hadn't spotted him yet.

Shit. They're going to try and get to the rock fissure on foot and cut me off.

He knew if that happened, he'd be picked apart on this mesa.

Mercer was about to stand when he caught a glimpse of something not far from where the SUV was heading. Through the scope, he spotted Angela's work vehicle, its white rooftop glinting in the sun like a homing beacon.

He traced a path from her Suburban up a slope that led towards a jagged escarpment of basalt along the west side of Black Canyon just a few yards down from the fissure. He caught a glimpse of Angela's green hat bobbing along the trail before it disappeared.

Where the hell is she going?

He felt his pulse quicken, knowing that anyone inter-secting Crowe's path out here was going to be viewed as expendable. Mercer didn't know if it was by chance or design that Crowe and his men were heading towards Angela or if the man had surmised that it was the only route to the fissure.

Either way, she was about to be in the crosshairs, and Mercer knew that whatever happened to her would be on his conscience no matter how far he fled from Blayne.

He cinched down his shoulder straps then patted Luce on the side.

"Time to do some hunting, girl."

CHAPTER 20

THE BLACK SUV stopped beside the weathered Suburban, and Crowe and his four men quickly exited.

Atley was still at the cabin, handling overwatch on his computer, while Jiya was following Mercer's tracks to the north along the rim of Black Canyon.

As his team gathered their ARs and donned their tactical vests, Crowe tapped on his ear-mic, contacting Atley.

"We are about a mile south of the location where you indicated there was a brief glimpse of someone last night. Do you have any better satellite coverage?"

"It's still intermittent. There's some interference or something in the upper atmosphere, maybe that storm that's rolling in, which is causing reception issues on my end."

"Well, what's the last thing you picked up on the two subjects moving in this direction?"

"Looks like they are heading south along the rim still. That was as of ninety minutes ago."

Crowe pushed his sunglasses further up on the bridge of

his nose then removed a shemagh from his pack, wrapping it around his neck and sliding part of the fabric up over his mouth to keep out the blowing grit.

"We're parked next to a vehicle that says Palladium Industries on the side; it belongs to that woman the sheriff told me about, Angela Owens. She's supposed to be a friend of Mercer's…a real good friend, I'm guessing, based upon how squirrely the sheriff was when I questioned him. Pull up everything you can on her."

Crowe glanced back at the road. "We ran into her field techs on the drive in, and they indicated she was coming up this way to grab some equipment, so maybe me and the boys will have a real friendly visit with Ms. Owens."

"Copy that, but just a reminder that we need to get what we came for and get out before the sheriff and his guys get more suspicious than they already are or the real Feds get wind of what happened to those two agents we eliminated in Durango."

"I ain't too worried about Dewey. He seems like the kinda guy who needs help tyin' his shoes. Besides, if my old pal Hendrix is nearby, this girlfriend of his will be of use in luring him right to us. I just hope that…"

Splinters of bone and red mist sprayed onto the ground near Crowe's boots as the merc standing by the rear hatch collapsed to the ground, the right side of his skull shattered.

Crowe dropped behind the rear wheel, removing his Glock just as he heard a sickeningly familiar thud, followed by another of his henchmen flopping onto the sand as blood and spinal fluid leaked out from the gaping wound below his left ear.

"Talk to me!" he said to the two remaining mercenaries, who had lunged for cover behind the waist-high boulders skirting the road.

"Shots came from the south," said the bearded man closest to him.

"No shit. That's where Hendrix is at, dumbass." He tapped on his ear-mic again. "Atley, I've got two men down. Find me a target."

"Working on it," said his second-in-command.

CHAPTER 21

MERCER EXAMINED his handiwork through the MK12's scope: the last two .308 rounds had effectively punched lethal holes through their intended targets.

He'd hoped one of the full-metal jacket rounds would have gone downrange into Deacon's caveman skull, but his former colleague was out of sight on the other side of the vehicle.

He glanced beyond the SUV, seeing a shallow drainage that wound up towards the fissure. He knew Crowe would have a half-mile of cover as he made his way to Angela's location.

She must have heard the gunshot and commotion by now and has taken cover somewhere.

Mercer slid back, coming into a squat then scanning the terrain to his rear for any signs of movement, knowing that the mantracker from last night had just gotten a fix on his exact location.

If he's out there, he's a fucking ghost.

There was nothing visible, and he couldn't waste any more time in getting to the fissure.

Nick glanced down at Luce, who was immediately at his side as she sprung out from beneath the juniper tree, trotting through a smattering of barrel-sized boulders dotting the terrain.

"Let's get Angela then drop the hell off this mesa to somewhere with better protection."

Mercer and the dog wove through the maze of brush and rock spires until he was thirty feet from the fissure. He caught a glimpse of red hair beneath a brimmed hat as Angela raised her head, peering out from a natural shelter of angled basalt that jutted from an escarpment along Black Canyon.

"Psst." He waved his hand at her, grateful she was alright.

Her eyes widened as she waved back.

"What the hell you doing out here?" he said, alternating his gaze between her and the trail to the right that led down to the vehicles.

"Me? What the fuck are you doing, Nick. Is that even your actual name? Dewey told me you're wanted by the FBI for killin' a bunch of innocent villagers in Africa."

Mercer sighed. "That's all bullshit. And those guys aren't Feds. They're mercenaries led by a guy named Deacon Crowe."

"Oh yeah, well, how come..."

He raised a finger to his lips. "Just be quiet and follow me down below. There's an old mineshaft we can take cover in. I'll explain everything."

He could see she was weighing the information, glancing between him and the trail back to the vehicles.

"Those guys are monsters," Nick said. "You go down there and they'll torture you to get to me and then slit your throat when they're all done. I know that guy Crowe, and he'll destroy anything in his way to get what he wants."

She gave him a hard stare. "And what about you? I thought you were just a woodworker. What will you destroy to get away?"

"Only those who would bring harm to you or Luce."

He glanced to the left, a scowl forming.

Crowe will get what's coming to him, either here in this desert or in the months ahead when I put him down for good.

"Alright. I'll come with you...for now," she said. "But I'm keeping you in front of me."

"That's fine. You're making the right decision."

"Not sure about that yet. But I don't want Luce getting corrupted any further by you."

CHAPTER 22

CROWE SUCKED IN A DEEP BREATH, gazing at the two dead men near the rear bumper. These were guys that had been with him from the early days when he joined Rohrbach's mercenary army in Sierra Leone. Hardy, reliable fighters. He tried to recall their last names but just shook his head, cursing at the reduction in manpower he'd suffered.

If I didn't need Hendrix alive, I'd just strafe this whole fucking mesa right now.

He heard Atley's voice crackle into his earpiece.

"I've got reception again, but Hendrix and the dog are nowhere in sight. They must have dropped below the rim or be hiding under a ledge."

"And the woman? Is she even out here?"

"She was. At least I think it was her. There was a lone individual a half-mile up from you, by that split in the canyon."

Crowe sighed, wishing he had air support and could get eyes down in that canyon. "She must have heard the shooting and taken cover."

Crowe clicked off, his ears now straining for sounds in

the distance, but the wind was too fierce. Glancing to the edge of the road, he saw a shallow drainage choked with brush and traced it towards the canyon.

He suspected Mercer wasn't going to waste time in a sniper's stakeout and was continuing along his evasion route in the gorge below.

Crowe leaned back towards his other two men. "Get the case out with those mini-drones. I want to get to that canyon and send one down below. The wind shouldn't be as bad there, and I want eyes on what's ahead."

CHAPTER 23

IT WAS JUST after 8 AM when the deputy drove into the Badger Gulch parking area. Dewey stepped out from the shade of a box elder tree, where he had been glassing the ridges with his binoculars. From what he knew, Mercer and Luce were nowhere near this area, but he was on edge and felt it necessary to inspect every noise behind him.

The deputy hastily exited his vehicle, leaving his car door open and trotting towards Dewey, his face drained of color.

"Sir, you're not going to believe this, but I got through on the HAM radio at Matt's place this morning. The FBI dispatcher in Durango said that those two agents whose names you gave me never reported in to work yesterday. The Bureau is searching for them as we speak."

Dewey's cheeks grew taut. "God, I knew something was way off."

"The agent in charge that I spoke with also said there's no one by the name of Crowe or Atley working for the Bureau."

"Did you fill them in on what was going on here?"

"Briefly. They're going to send a team here this afternoon, maybe later, as they've got personnel spread all over the field searching for their missing agents."

Dewey rested his hand on his pistol, pacing back and forth. "Did you notice if any of Crowe's guys are still manning the roadblocks?"

The young deputy shook his head. "No, they're gone. They just placed a bunch of orange barrels and cones across the road that they got from our transportation yard."

Dewey clenched his teeth. "They must've narrowed down where Nick is at and are going after him."

"Sir, maybe we should call the sheriff's department up in Blanding and Monticello and tell him what's going on. We could use more manpower."

"Not a chance. Sheriff Cooper and his storm troopers would just implement martial law in Blayne. Plus, he's got a helluva itchy trigger finger, and we've got enough psychos with delusions of justice running around here right now."

Dewey headed towards his vehicle with the young deputy in tow. "Is Deputy Rawlins still at the other trailhead parking lot?"

"Yes, sir. I spoke with him briefly after leaving Matt's place. He was thinking of heading to the south roadblock to redirect traffic since those other fellas left."

"All right, leave him be for now. I need you to follow me over to Mercer's cabin. I want to see if that other guy Atley is still there or if they left anything behind that might indicate what they're planning next."

The drive to the cabin took less than ten minutes. When Dewey pulled his vehicle into the parking area beside Mercer's toolshed, he noted that there was only one SUV there. The thrashing of the wind had obliterated any tracks in the dirt, and he assumed that Atley or whoever was still inside hadn't left the cabin since last night.

Stepping out of his vehicle, he waited for the young deputy to exit his patrol car then used a hand motion to signal that he should go around the back.

Dewey cleared his throat and pulled his shoulders back, fighting the urge to vomit as he walked towards the front porch. Heading up the steps, he removed the retention clasp on the holster of his Sig P226 pistol.

He lingered on the porch for a few seconds, waiting for his deputy to work his way around the backside. When Dewey had determined it was time, he slowly opened the front door, proceeding inside.

Atley was still seated at the kitchen table, fixated on his laptop. Beside his computer was a Glock 17.

"Not a good time, Sheriff. We are closing in on this nutjob Mercer, and I need all my attention on my front sights."

"Where's he at? Mercer?"

"By Black Canyon and this huge crack on the west side. We'll have him bagged shortly then be out of your hair."

Dewey kept waiting to see his deputy appear in the window of the rear door, wondering where the man was.

Atley slowly removed his headset, putting it down on the table, then positioned his hands by the front of the laptop. His gaze turned towards the sheriff, his eyes settling on Dewey's right hand, which was resting atop his Sig P226 pistol. "Somethin' on your mind, Sheriff?"

Dewey felt like he was a boxer about to be backed into a corner for a vicious beating unless he acted fast.

He began withdrawing his pistol. "Just slide back from the desk and put your hands up. It's over. I know you're not a federal agent."

"You're right, Sheriff. Crowe and I are with the CIA, and you're interfering with our apprehension of a rogue agent."

Dewey had his Sig leveled at the man's chest. "The CIA doesn't go around kidnapping federal agents and assuming their identities."

"Oh, you'd be surprised what's done in the name of national security." Atley stood up, raising his hands.

"Turn around." Dewey removed his handcuffs with his left hand, moving towards Atley as the man complied.

"Is any of that horseshit you told me about Mercer even true?"

"Does it matter?"

"It does to me."

"Well, let's just say he has something that we want, and our boss is willing to pay me and Crowe a lot of money to bend a few rules."

Dewey kept his pistol pointed at the man's back as his left hand moved in to cuff the man's wrist. As soon as the first cuff was partly wrapped in place, Atley ducked slightly then spun, sending a vicious forearm strike into Dewey's head.

The blow knocked the sheriff off balance. Atley drove a shin kick into the sheriff's groin then sent a right hook into Dewey's face. Dewey hit the floor hard, giving Atley enough time to spring towards the table for his Glock.

As Dewey regained his footing and pivoted around, the splintering sound of a single gunshot echoed throughout the cabin. Atley fell against the table as shards of bone and blood spilled from the side of his head. The man slid to the ground, collapsing in a heap.

Dewey's eyes darted wildly around the cabin, finally settling on a shadow by the side window. Beyond a single hole in the glass was his deputy.

"Sorry, Sheriff. There was too much debris along this side to make it quietly to the back door, so I had to wait here."

Dewey sucked in a deep breath, steadying his legs as he glanced at the young deputy then over to Atley's body. "Wes, you got nothing to apologize for."

The young deputy disappeared for a second then came walking in through the front door, still clutching his duty pistol.

Dewey walked up to the dead man, noticing the well-placed shot in the left temple. "That's some fine shootin', son." He glanced at the deputy's hands, noticing an absence of the tremors afflicting his own. "You can be my backup any day, Wes."

"Thank you, sir."

He thrust his chin towards the back door. "Why don't you make a sweep outside in case any of Crowe's guys are still around and heard the gunshot. I'm gonna see what's on this laptop."

The deputy nodded then headed to the back porch. Dewey grabbed a small hand towel from the bathroom and used it to wipe the droplets of blood off the laptop screen.

He sat down, his insides queasy from the kick below the belt. Dewey removed a couple of Tums from the half-used roll in his pocket then chomped down the antacids, hoping it would calm the cauldron in his stomach as he stared at the two red blips on the screen, which had just joined with another before disappearing into Black Canyon.

CHAPTER 24

"THE HELO with our snatch-and-grab team will be arriving at the airfield in Blanding within the hour. That's just a half-hour or so northeast of Blayne," said Director Neil Patterson.

Ryland glanced at his watch. "That should put us on the ground there in two hours." He looked out the window at the monotonous plains of Kansas. "The pilot here said there's supposed to be a helluva windstorm brewing in the Four Corners area. I'm not sure how far our helo is going to get if it turns into a full-blown sandstorm."

Patterson turned his tablet around, showing a topographic map of Blayne. "I've already got a few sites picked out. One is just four miles south of the town in a U-shaped valley, which should provide some protection from the elements. There are a few level spots that should suffice."

He studied Ryland's face, seeing a faint bead of sweat above the man's upper lip. "There's some Dramamine in the bathroom."

The portly man licked his lips. "Nah, I should be good. That vending food machine I grabbed at the hangar before we left isn't settling well." He thrust his chin out the window. "Besides, landing on some mesa in the desert during a storm doesn't sound very safe, regardless of how flat the ground is."

Patterson frowned. "Mesas are always flat; the term is Spanish for table. Have you ever spent time in the desert, Ryland...any desert?"

"I was once at a FOB in Afghanistan for a few weeks. The rest of my time was in the tropics of West Africa, as you know."

"You worked under David Hastings briefly, the case officer who covered Sierra Leone and Liberia, isn't that right?"

Rylan nodded. "Rickety old bastard."

"Yes, he was, but he was also a hell of an operator in his younger days."

"You knew him?"

"We came up together in the Agency after being in the same class at the Farm. Dave was eventually assigned to West Africa while I was in the north of the country, Algeria and Egypt mainly."

"Yeah, well, his past eventually caught up with him. From what I heard, that car bomb in Guinea vaporized him in seconds. So much for being a helluva operator."

Patterson gave the stout man a piercing stare. "As I recall, you took over his post after his untimely death."

"That's correct. I was already in-country and knew the region better than most."

"Even better than the men and women already working for years under Hastings?"

"They were field agents who didn't know shit about politics or the bigger picture of what we were trying to do in that country."

"Like trying to stop Rohrbach's tentacles from invading every corner of West Africa?" Again, Patterson scrutinized the man's tense face. Ryland fidgeted in his seat like an animal with its paw caught in a wire snare. He knew the man had probably covered his tracks in Sierra Leone, and while Patterson had no solid proof, he was sure Ryland was somehow connected to Rohrbach's shady dealings.

Ryland looked up and down the aisle, his eyes settling on the bathroom door at the rear. "Think I'll grab some Dramamine after all." The pudgy man unbuckled, heading to the rear.

Once he heard the bathroom door lock, Patterson removed his iPhone, sending a brief text message then noticing it had bounced back for the second time since the flight had departed Virginia.

He dialed his intel desk at Langley, the familiar voice of his head analyst, Lynn Vogel, coming over the speaker. She had been Patterson's chief targeter, tracking down the locations of terrorists, jihadist leaders and bomb-makers for the Special Activities Division agents and most recently starting the transition to overseeing intel for a relatively new Search and Destroy Unit.

What Patterson's elite field agents possessed in tradecraft, Vogel held in spades with her targeting and analysis abilities.

"I need to know why I can't get a message out to Blayne," he said.

"Let me see what I can find, sir," Vogel replied.

A few minutes later, her voice returned. "There appears to be some kind of comms blackout over the entire town. It's not internal...the cell towers seem to be functioning."

"Then someone is running deliberate interference. A hacker perhaps?"

The sound of more typing followed as the woman was busy on her laptop. "Correct, sir. I'm detecting a jamming signal that is skewing the two cell-tower relays in that region of Utah."

"I need you to track down the source and eliminate it. In the meantime, I'll text you the message I'm trying to send. Run that through SAT-COMs. I need it to reach its destination."

"I'm on it. There's something else that just came across my screen, sir. The FBI office in Durango is mobilizing a tac-response team and will be departing for Blayne in a few hours."

"Shit. We need to be on our way out of there before they arrive. Track their movements and keep me posted on their ETA in Utah."

"Copy that, sir."

Patterson needed to be on the ground in Blayne *now*. He couldn't risk having the Feds find out that the CIA was conducting an operation stateside. The fallout back in D.C. would be a disaster for the Agency, not to mention a potential career-ender for Patterson.

He tapped on his tablet screen, checking on the departure time of his grab team enroute to Blanding, Utah. At least they were on schedule. They'd put down Crowe once and for all.

Patterson glanced back at the bathroom. *And maybe Ryland will accidentally miss his flight back from that unforgiving desert.*

CHAPTER 25

Whitman Airfield

CIA operative Joshua Brins had just returned five hours ago from a mission in Panama and had been looking forward to a few days off with his family when he received a call from Director of Clandestine Operations Neil Patterson before his Agency jet departed Virginia.

He'd only ever spoken once to the director, and it was when he had become team leader last year. During that discussion, Brins received the rundown on his role, evasion protocols for overseas missions, leads for selecting his own contractors, and his utter deniability as one of Patterson's hitmen.

When he answered the director's call this morning, he knew it wasn't going to be a congratulatory message on the

Panama job. If Patterson was personally calling, then something urgent was required.

The three other men on his team were busy doing a weapons and gear inspection at the steel table in the corner of the small hangar near a black Bell 206 helicopter.

Brins stepped outside to have a smoke, scrolling again through the two images on his phone that Patterson had sent.

The first man had short black hair that looked like it was neatly styled and covered with gel, giving Brins the impression that the man worked for a modeling agency rather than formerly for an intelligence agency.

Deacon Crowe. Kill Order.

The name and face didn't ring a bell. Brins scrolled down to the next photo. The image looked older, showing a lean-faced man with a bit of scruff and a green shirt whose collar appeared to be soaked with sweat.

When he'd seen the photo earlier, Brins had paused, staring into the eyes as if he was standing across from Nathan Hendrix, an agent with the Special Activities Division that Brins had worked briefly with in Algeria years ago.

Only the name Patterson listed below this man's photo read Nicholas Mercer, followed by the words *Rogue Agent. MIA 5 Years. Capture Order.*

Brins knew it wasn't uncommon to have multiple aliases in this line of work, but why this guy Hendrix, or Mercer, was on Patterson's shit list was beyond him.

Hendrix had been a solid operator who had been a mentor of sorts following Brins' arrival in Algeria. He had even stuck his neck out for Brins' team a few weeks later, violating comms protocols to alert him that the road they were taking after a hostage rescue was potentially laced with IEDs despite what the intel desk at Langley was indicating.

Brins never did find out if that was the case, trusting Hendrix's intel over some deskbound analyst across the Atlantic. He diverted his team back to the extraction point along another route, but he'd heard later that Hendrix received a severe reprimand from his superiors at Langley and was reassigned to Liberia for his insubordination.

Now, we're supposed to bag up this guy Mercer and drop him where...in a black site?

But that was the job: dealing with bullshit orders and tidbits of information that often didn't reveal the entirety of the story. And he imagined that this guy Mercer had quite a story, if he was branded a rogue agent and had been on the run for years.

Just as he was about to put his phone away, it rang. He answered the unfamiliar number, hearing a bronchial voice on the other end.

"Agent Brins, this is Garrett Ryland, Senior Case Officer with the CIA. I have a business proposition for you that you are going to want to hear. But before I discuss that, you should know that your boss, Neil Patterson, is planning to burn you and your men following the mission in Blayne."

Brins narrowed his eyes, stabbing out his cigarette on the steel wall, listening intently to the man on the other end.

CHAPTER 26

THE TEMPERATURE HAD COOLED SIGNIFICANTLY since he had dropped below the rim. Mercer led the way as Angela kept her distance, staying ten feet behind him at all times. Trotting to her rear was Luce, who stopped occasionally to inspect the sandstone crevices for rock squirrels.

One mile in, Mercer emerged from the thick swath of immense cottonwoods lining the bottom of Black Canyon and made his way along a bighorn sheep trail, heading towards a square shadow two hundred feet up the sheer cliff face. The opening was barely visible, covered with a heavy blanket of wild grapevines and Virginia creeper.

The trail was only a foot wide, and he paused frequently to negotiate the more precarious sections of loose stones. Approaching the entrance, he peered into the square opening of a large mineshaft, hoping not to surprise a bobcat, or worse yet, a cougar.

Once he was sure the opening was free of critters or rattlesnakes, he walked inside. The first twenty feet were cavernous and had been used by miners as a common area to sleep, cook meals and store their equipment.

Beyond that was the tunnel that headed into the inky darkness.

Mercer set his pack down, removing a water bottle. He gulped down half the contents then scooped out a small basin in the sand, lining it with his ball cap and pouring the rest inside for Luce as he'd done countless times on their trips.

Angela remained by the opposite wall, leaning back with her arms crossed.

"You want to tell me what the hell is going on now?"

He started to move closer, but her outstretched hand told him to stay put.

"So, the gist of it is that five years ago, that guy up top Deacon Crowe and I were working for the CIA."

He paused, waiting for a reaction, but she only glared at him. "OK, sure. CIA. Got it."

"We were assigned to the Gola people, who are the natives living in the highlands of northwestern Liberia. This is a vast jungle region with an assortment of tribes in the mountains and ratty towns miles down below revolving around the diamond mining industry. Our job was to train the indigenous people to combat Liberian president Kananga's forces, whose goals, for lack of a better explanation, weren't aligned with U.S. foreign policy in the region.

"We were successful, and during the two-year period, the Gola tribe regained a lot of their traditional lands, some of which were suspected to be in diamond-rich valleys."

Mercer paced back and forth, keeping his rifle held low as he focused on the canyon floor below while recounting his story.

"Everything changed the following summer when there was an Ebola outbreak. It spread from the smaller towns in the central part of the country to the cities along the coast.

Prominent border crossings were sealed, and military lock-downs were issued. Given our secluded location in the high-lands, we were unaffected and thought that we would ride out the disease as villages had done in the past.

"Only Edgar Rohrbach, a diamond broker out of Johan-nesburg, used his private mercenary army to sweep in from the wilderness bordering Sierra Leone and target the diamond mines to the south of us. Pretty sure that mother-fucker and his family all sleep in coffins. They've been exploiting and manipulating people and politics in Africa for the past century to further their reach.

"Fortunately, when his goons descended on our valley, the Golas were the only sizeable force standing in his way. By this time, the Agency's commitment to the region had wavered. Kananga and several of his top advisors had died from the virus, and the military was in chaos with the country beginning to collapse into a failed state.

"When the virus first struck, we held the upper hand, since our indig fighters knew the travel routes in and out of those remote valleys, but one night, shelling commenced on our side of the mountain. Entire villages were decimated along with our arsenal." He stopped walking, his voice lowering. "Thousands were killed. Entire families shattered."

He ran his hand through his wavy hair as he glanced back into the inky passage. "Deacon had sold us out. Rohrbach or someone high up in the Sierra Leone govern-ment must have gotten to him...paid him off. Deacon...my brother-in-arms...my 'friend'"—he clawed out air quotes at the latter term—"had revealed all of our bases and travel corridors. The Golas never had a chance."

Angela leaned over to pet Luce, who had settled in next to her leg.

"I rallied the survivors, and we headed for two days on foot to the northern border with Guinea. We were hunted the entire way by Crowe's army of thugs, but me and thirty of my remaining men used guerilla tactics to buy the women and children some time. In the end, it was only myself and eight of my men who rejoined the others at the border.

"By then our government and my boss, a guy named Patterson, weren't interested in getting tied up in any political entanglements assisting a bunch of refugees in another country. So, I used my remaining Agency funds to bribe the border guards to let us cross into Guinea."

He retreated to the opposite wall, slumping against the side then sliding to the ground. The only sounds in the old mineshaft came from the unrelenting wind outside.

Angela stood up, moving closer to him. "That's a touching story, if it's true. I'm not sure what's real with you though. You told me when we first met that you had worked as a business consultant overseas. But you really worked for the CIA?" She shook her head, gritting her teeth. "You were a fucking spook?"

"It's the truth, Angie. I spent nearly a decade working in various African nations."

She slammed her boot into his hip. "You're a professional liar. Job well done. You accomplished your mission in making a fool out of me. Is your name even Nick Mercer?"

He didn't respond, averting his eyes.

Luce lifted her head, tilting it to the side as she glanced between both the humans. Angela came over and squatted down beside the dog, caressing her neck. "Luce, you're the only good thing to come out of him bein' in Blayne."

"I get you're pissed. I never wanted to lie to you, Angie. I didn't call you after we were together the other night because I just didn't want to continue leading a double life with you...deceiving you about who I am." He waved out to the canyon. "I figured you'd be packing your bags soon anyway, moving on to another job."

"No, don't put that shit on me. You're the sole reason we're sitting in this musty tunnel right now with a bunch of Feds...or mercenaries...or whoever the hell they are after us."

"Well, putting you in harm's way was never my intention."

Angela lowered her head against her scrunched knees.

"I was careful during all my time living here. The only actual town I ever went to was Moab, and I knew all the points of vulnerability with the few street cams there."

"And you chose Blayne because of its remoteness or just to ruin my life?"

"Eddie Peshlakai, actually. He and I served together in the army when I first joined. We eventually went our own ways...him going into artillery at Fort Sill and me getting recruited by the Agency after my special-forces days. We kept in touch over the years, and he always offered me an invite if I ever needed to get off the grid. He's the only person alive who knows about my real identity."

She raised an eyebrow. "Well, his little ranch is about as off the grid as a person can get in this world."

"Shortly before I fled Liberia, that guy Patterson I mentioned who was my training officer at the Agency sent me a message saying that the CIA had put out a burn notice on me."

"Was that because you blew all their money getting those survivors out of Liberia?"

He flared his eyebrows. "Hmm...you think?"

"You said you arrived in Blayne four years ago, but the events in Liberia were five years back. What happened in between?"

"I fled from Africa, bouncing around the world for about eleven months, planning out my next move. It's not easy erasing your past and taking on another identity, no matter how fabricated it all is. My dad was a carpenter, and I grew up in the trade, so I figured being a woodworker wasn't going to be a stretch. I just needed a base and figured the Four Corners is pretty damn remote, so I made my way to Eddie's place a few hours south of here. He helped me get my feet back on the ground and eventually told me about the cabin for sale in Blayne."

"And you bought that with leftover cash from the CIA?"

"I'm no thief...not in the traditional sense of that word, anyway. All that money went to the survivors who made it across the border. But before I disappeared from Africa, I hit one of Rohrbach's smaller diamond smuggling convoys on the border of Sierra Leone. Those stones helped me start a new life while dishing out some payback to that son of a bitch."

Her fierce stare softened slightly. Just recounting his past to someone felt like he'd shrugged a few hundred pounds of stress from his neck and shoulders.

A faint crackling sound emanated from Angela's backpack. She opened the side pouch, removing her two-way radio.

"I shouldn't be getting a signal down here. This works off the repeater towers up top."

Mercer stood up, staring out at the tunnel opening. "Unless someone has the means of boosting that signal or creating another relay point." He grabbed the radio, turning up the volume.

"Blue Ridge, this is K2, do you copy?" Mercer felt an icy chill sweep through the mineshaft as he recalled the old Agency call signs he and Deacon Crowe used during countless operations in Africa.

"Repeat, Blue Ridge, do you copy, this is K2, over."

He glanced up at Angela's taut face as the static ensued.

"Come on, buddy, we can talk," Crowe said. "This is a secure channel. And I've missed working with you all these years, Nate...or, I mean, Nick."

Mercer moved the radio closer, as if he was staring at an evil talisman, while Crowe continued.

"You're not still sore about your native pals going up in smoke in the jungle, are you? That was just business, nothing personal."

He clutched the radio. "Tell me, Deke, how much did Rohrbach slip into your pocket to betray all of us, mother-fucker? To betray all of the people we were sent to help."

"It was more than a handful of silver dollars, I can tell you that, buddy. After living on rice and yams for a year in those rathole villages we were assigned to, I decided a change was in order."

"You condemned a lot of lives when you sold us out. Do you know the damage you did, or were those artillery strikes called in from the comfort of your bungalow along the coast? You orphaned thousands of kids and destroyed entire communities that had been around for generations."

"Hang on a second while I get some Kleenex. Come on, dude...that's a way of life over there. Hell, even when we worked up in Algeria, every other kid on the street was an orphan who had lost his parents in a car bombing or a fucking coup." He laughed. "Your eyes were always glazed over with a patriotic haze. It's why everyone rallied to you. You were like a high priest who was going to lift them out of their misery. Me, I knew the political winds would change one day, and the same Agency who sent us to train the natives would be supporting a rival warlord next door in a few years."

"We were there to change that, not to add to the horror. But the crisis in faith you clearly had after a bag of cash was tossed in your lap must have made you forget that."

"It was a bag of diamonds, actually. But hell, that's all ancient history now. And if it wasn't for your forged documents turning up on Hassan's laptop this past spring, you could probably have spent your days playing Jeremiah Johnson up here with that gingey babe you just rescued."

Angela's eyes narrowed. He slid back a few feet, expecting another kick, while she glanced up at the rock ceiling, cursing aloud.

"How about we meet up, Deke? Just you and me, settle this, man to man, unless you've forgotten what that means."

"How about you just turn over those red diamonds and we'll call it good."

"I have no idea what you're talking about."

"Rohrbach thinks otherwise since he's studied the satellite footage from that hit you did on his convoy in great detail."

"I only took a small pouch of raw diamonds, divvying it up with my men and taking a few small stones for myself... but, you know, it's a shame you came all this way for nothing. The good news is that it's only a five-hour drive to the Grand Canyon from here, so you should consider doing some sightseeing on your return trip to whatever cesspool you crawled out of."

"Amigo, you really want to add your girlfriend to the long list of bullet-riddled bodies you have on your record?

You already whacked four of my guys, and that's really going to count against you at the pearly gates someday."

"You must be losin' it in your old age. I only smoked three of your rent-a-soldiers."

"Pff, whatever. Just give me those red diamonds and all of this goes away. I'll even tell Rohrbach that you took a bad fall over a cliff. Then you can run off again and start over in some other one-cow town."

He clenched his jaw, scanning the opposite rim of the canyon. "You recall that old special-ops trainer at the Farm who had been in Vietnam?"

"Spacey or something. What about him?"

"Spivey, actually. Remember how he told the story about being hunted for days by a small group of VC after his recon mission went to shit? He finally decided he'd had enough and button-hooked around them one night, taking out their sentry then gutting the hell out of the other guys while they slept."

Mercer flicked off the radio, tossing it onto Angela's lap. He clutched his rifle, moving beside the opening and peering down canyon.

"Where are you headed? You can't be serious about going after those guys?" she said.

"Crossed my mind, but right now, it'll keep them on edge if they think I'm coming." He raised his rifle, peering through the scope, slowly sweeping from right to left above the treetops then in the direction of the fissure. A minute later, he stood motionless, focusing his scope's red dot on the target.

A faint gunshot rang out from the suppressed rifle, followed by a Frisbee-sized drone splintering apart and raining down upon the trees. He scanned up and down the canyon one more time before returning to Luce and Angela.

"We won't be getting any more calls from Deacon," he said, resting his arm on Luce as she leaned into his side.

"Didn't that just give away our location?"

"No, not immediately, anyway. The drone was making a pass along the opposite side of the canyon, and there are dozens of small caves and old tunnels in these parts. If he knew we were here, it would have been hovering right outside the entrance."

"So, this guy Deacon...he was a friend at one time?"

He sighed, rubbing the back of his neck. "I thought so. We came up together at the Agency and were assigned to North Africa for a few years before being tasked with counter-insurgency efforts in Liberia."

"And you just overlooked the fact that he was a lunatic?"

"He was a flawed individual, for sure, but he had my back plenty of times over the years. And when you run through a shit-ton of bullets on a regular basis, you lean on the operators around you." He tilted his head back, closing his eyes. "I just never figured he would sell us all out."

"Well, now what? What's your plan, Nick Mercer? I have a decent, if seasonal, job here and would like to keep coming back in the near future. Your setting up shop in Blayne may have been a convenient way to hide out from your past, but I've really come to like the people, and now you've brought a bunch of sociopaths to their door."

"He only wants me so he can locate the diamonds, and since they only have a small cadre of guys, it's going to be hard to contain this area. They're a snatch-and-grab team who need to get me then get the hell out of here before the real FBI shows up and shuts down the region."

"What diamonds?" she said.

"It's a long story."

"Well, is it worth dying for...or me dying for? I'm not

connected with any of this, so just give them to him so he'll leave."

"It's not that simple."

"Most long stories aren't."

"I don't have those red diamonds on me."

She held up her hands. "God, don't tell me they're back at your cabin somewhere."

"It doesn't matter. Even if I gave those up, and I won't, Deke is a ruthless son of a bitch who would still try and collect on Rohrbach's bounty on me. This won't end until both of them are boots up. Besides, I've been working on an idea for some time on how to funnel the funds from those diamonds back to Liberia so it benefits the people there rather than the Rohrbachs of the world."

His eyes darted along the dusty ground. "Aside from their significant monetary value, Rohrbach probably also wants those particular diamonds so his lab guys can identify their specific molecular properties which will allow him to narrow down which of the hundreds of jungle valleys the stones came from. After that, he will destroy everyone and everything in his way to control that region, making the recent civil wars in West Africa pale in comparison."

He retrieved his rifle, pointing the barrel down the mineshaft. "Right now, we need to get moving. First, I'm going to check for rattlesnakes, then we're going to walk down the length of this tunnel for a quarter-mile and veer off to a small passage on the left for two hundred yards. There's a vertical shaft heading to the surface we can take. I stowed a rope ladder there a few months back."

"You're forgetting the rockpile blocking the tunnel a few hundred yards down. I surveyed this place last month."

"I know. I created *that* small rockpile with a small shape-charge of C4 on the sidewall a while back. I didn't want you or anyone else messing with the cache of supplies I buried back there."

She licked her lip. "You screwed with a historic archeology site? How many other sites out here have you tampered with?"

"Yeah, I know. Why risk running afoul of the law...you're not going to report me, are you?"

"Shut up, asshole. I still haven't decided if I'll ever forgive you for lying to me."

———

DEACON and two of his shooters squatted a few feet from the rim of Black Canyon, gazing down below with their rifle scopes then up towards the opposite side.

When he was done, he tapped on his ear-mic, contacting Rohrbach's cyber-division, who were operating the company's proprietary satellite.

"Tell me you have something on Hendrix's location." He wiped some grit from his cheek.

"We did until he slipped down into that maze of trees below." A few seconds of frantic typing followed before the young man's voice returned. "I'm not seeing anything on thermals, so they must be under a ledge or maybe in a cave."

"That woman, Owens, she's a mining inspector...they could be inside one of the old tunnels down here; she probably knows them all. Pull up everything from the government land agencies out here and see what shows up for mineshafts within a one-mile radius of our location."

"Copy that, sir. I'll get back with you if I find something."

"There's no *if*, you asshole. Find where the hell they're at ASAFP."

Deacon swiveled around, glancing past his remaining mercenaries, who were spread out on either side of him.

Shit, if Hendrix is in a mineshaft with another exit, he could outflank us or end up outside of our search radius…or just play out his colorful story and buttonhook around us.

But Crowe figured that Mercer would be hampered by the presence of the woman and the dog and would now be focused on gaining distance from his pursuers rather than staging an ambush.

He pivoted back towards Black Canyon, which had become an obstacle he hadn't planned on. "There's not enough dead grass to create a wildfire to smoke 'em out, and we're going to be targets in a shooting gallery if we walk down the center of that canyon." He scanned the opposite ridge.

He nudged his boot against the leg of the merc on his right. "Hakim, I want you to get our remaining drones hovering just below the rim, scouting for any caves or tunnels."

"With these high winds, we risk losing them against the rocks."

"Fuck the winds. We risk losing Hendrix, and then this whole mission was for nothing. Get going."

"Yes, sir."

Deacon glanced at the other henchman to his right, who was lying prone with a Remington 700 rifle. "If the opportunity for a leg shot on either the woman or that dog presents itself, take it. That'll slow them down enough to give us an edge. But under no circumstances is Hendrix to be wounded. I need that prick alive. Once he's in my possession, I'll peel him apart until he gives up the location of the diamonds."

CHAPTER 27

THE FIRST FIVE hundred yards of crouch-walking through the mineshaft was slow going, as the ceiling was at an angle, giving Mercer just enough clearance to avoid raking his head open on the jagged rock.

He paused in the center of the shaft, glancing back at Luce then Angela at the rear as his headlamp illuminated the murky passage. "You ever wear a mask when you're down in these old tunnels?" he said to Angela.

"No. There's no methane or deadly gases."

He pointed to the copious amounts of rodent droppings on either side of the passage.

Angela's eyes widened. "Shit."

"You got that right...decades of it. That's why I asked about the masks." He gave her a puzzled expression, wondering why she didn't know that. "Hantavirus is spread through deer mice droppings and can get into your lungs in seconds."

"My boss didn't go over that. He just handed me the keys to the Suburban and sent me on my way. Besides, I've mostly been doing surface surveys and don't get down into these old shafts much because of the dangers of collapse."

He shone his light along the length of the passage up ahead. "Just stay directly behind me and you won't stir up any of the droppings."

"And if a person gets hantavirus...what then?"

"Your lungs fill with fluid, and there's a fifty percent mortality rate and no cure, so either you're a lucky bastard and survive or you hope that the Grim Reaper drops in for an early visit at the hospital."

"That's uplifting. Not sure I'm glad I asked...and not sure why the hell people like living in the desert anyway, given all the things that can kill you."

"You're right...it's safer in the city."

"Shut up."

Ten minutes later, they arrived at a pile of rubble. Mercer removed his pack then began moving rocks from the upper section near the curved ceiling. "This was meant only to deter any curiosity seekers who might venture in here, so the rocks don't go back that far. We just need to clear away a few feet off the top then we can shimmy through."

Angela stroked the dog's side for a few seconds then moved past her and began helping Mercer pluck the football-sized rocks away.

After they had cleared close to sixteen inches of space, Mercer shoved his pack and rifle beyond the opening then crawled through while Luce followed on his heels. Angela mimicked the same moves, wriggling up then down the narrow crevice.

Once they were on the other side, Mercer removed three glo-sticks from his pack, activating them then tossing each on the ground along the left side of the tunnel.

Angela flicked debris off her red ponytail then leaned back against the passageway. "By how relaxed Luce is, I'd say you two have done this more than once."

"Yeah, twice a year, actually. I have a couple of caches hidden in the tunnels and overhangs in this canyon and Gould Canyon."

"Aren't you worried about some hunter or hiker coming across them?"

He shook his head. "You ever meet Dwight...the old guy with long white hair who runs the farmer's market on Sundays at the lodge?"

"Yeah, I've seen him. Never talked to him though."

"He used to do all the adobe work on the older homes in these parts. Guy grew up in New Mexico and built adobe and strawbale homes for a living. I spent my first summer helping him out on his place, as his back had a few too many miles on it, and I wanted to learn how to do stone masonry and adobe."

She wiped the dust off her nose. "This is a fascinating story about the history of architecture in the Southwest... what's your point, and why can't you ever fucking respond with a direct answer?"

"To return to your question about someone stumbling across my caches, the *answer* is...not likely," he said, extending a spear hand just beyond her left shoulder.

She pivoted, gazing at the wall of rock and dried mud that resembled the rest of the tunnel they'd been crawling through.

Mercer returned to the base of the rockpile, lifting a flat slab of sandstone and removing a steel-headed mallet and metal chisel. He tugged on Angela's shirt sleeve, motioning for her to move.

Mercer placed the flat chisel tip onto the adobe, chinking between two rocks in the wall, then began forcefully striking the earthen material until it cracked apart.

He performed this same routine along a rectangular pattern over a one-square-foot area. When he was done, he set the mallet down and used the chisel as a pry bar to remove a fist-sized rock from the top. Once that was out of the way, he pulled free the remaining rocks, exposing a knee-deep pocket in the wall.

Mercer lifted up a blue tarp, revealing a canvas rucksack that he slid out into the faint light of the green glo-sticks.

"You gonna get into a new set of clothes so you can look spiffy...is that why we came this way?" she said.

He smirked. "I already look spiffy. Most of the items in here are just to replenish supplies or were just in case I had fled my cabin without my gear for some reason."

Mercer removed a couple of spare pistol and rifle magazines, 550 cord, a Mora knife, a spark rod, water purification tablets, a small cooking pot and a few other survival-related items, setting them down on the blue tarp beside him. Next, he pulled out a square steel contraption and a large set of pliers.

"What's that for?" she said, staring at the unusual item as Luce curled up next to her leg.

"Conibear trap. Most people around these parts use them for trapping beaver or raccoon...but they'll snap a person's humerus or tibia in half just as well."

He shuffled on his knees back towards the base of the rockpile, scooping out a layer of sand in the middle until there was a three-inch depression. He glanced back at Angela. "Why don't you back up about ten feet and make sure to keep Luce by your side while I set this."

She crouch-walked down the passageway, the only visible slivers of light coming from a small tunnel to the left where the vertical shaft heading to the surface was located.

In the past, Mercer had used the smaller book-sized #110 Conibear bodygrip traps to kill unwanted rodents in the rafters of his tool shed and attic. Those were easily set by hand, but this was a #330 Conibear that was triple the size of its smaller counterpart and required the use of a specialized set of pliers to clamp down the heavy-duty springs while the deadly trap was set.

Mercer set the folded trap down then placed the tips of the oversized pliers on either side of the two frames that were joined in the middle by round hinges. He heaved his upper body into the movement, exerting his arms as he separated the two frames in the opposite direction, leaving the pliers clamped in place to keep them from shifting.

Next, he flipped the small trigger mechanism over one end of the frame. Sticking out from the trigger were two thin but rigid wires. He spread apart the ten-inch wires so they spanned the gap in the middle of the framework.

After he'd finished, he carefully set the trap flat in the depression then slowly removed the pliers. The trigger mechanism would keep the trap from springing until something or someone stepped onto the two wires, releasing 330 pounds per inch of force upon their limb.

Mercer sifted handfuls of sand over the trap, cloaking the presence of the bone-splintering device.

He shuffled back, retrieving the other items from the blue tarp then stuffing the empty dufflebag into the rock crevice in the wall. He didn't bother covering it, figuring it would serve as a visual distraction from the ground by the trap to whomever was climbing over the rockpile.

He grabbed his MK12 leaning against the wall then headed towards the dog and the woman, who had already begun moving in the direction of the sunlight in the leftward passage.

CHAPTER 28

Deacon's earpiece crackled. "Sir, I triangulated the gunshot that took out the mini-drone and collated that with records on old tunnels in the area from hacking the U.S. Bureau of Mines' database. There is a site about a mile south of that fissure where you're at. That must be where they are, since thermals aren't showing anyone moving along the canyon floor."

"That's the best news I've heard since we got out to this sandbox. Any word on Atley or Jiya? They haven't checked in, and I can't reach either of them."

"No, sir. I still show Atley's computer as being online, but Jiya is MIA. I will do a visual sweep of the canyon rim if you'd like."

"Forget it. His comms might be down, or maybe he took a fall and broke his fucking neck. Keep your eyes trained on our location for Hendrix."

CHAPTER 29

Fifteen minutes later, Mercer broke through the old boards over the top of the vertical passage. He poked his head out, quickly scanning the terrain, then emerged, moving towards a thumb-sized rock spire to the left. He used his rifle scope to glass to the north and west. From his location, he saw Angela's Suburban and the black SUV a mile to the right.

With no movement in sight, he figured Crowe and his remaining guys were down in Black Canyon. Assuming they found the old mineshaft, Mercer figured he only had about a thirty-minute lead on his pursuers, and he, Luce and Angela still needed to trot overland to Gould Canyon then drop below. From there it would be a short jaunt to the San Juan River, where he had another concealed cache. This one was larger, containing an inflatable kayak and a few other critical supplies.

The only problem was that it was only suitable for one person. He figured Luce, weighing only thirty-five pounds, wouldn't be an issue.

Fuck, another reason to be single. Too much baggage in life just slows your stride.

He would worry about Angela's fate when the time came. Right now, he needed to extract Luce from the mine. He crouch-walked back to the opening, setting his pack and rifle down then removing his climbing harness and rope. He dropped it down to Angela, who went about lashing it on the dog the way Mercer had described earlier.

CHAPTER 30

BLANDING, Utah

TWENTY-TWO MILES NORTHEAST of Blayne

PATTERSON HASTILY TROTTED across the small airfield towards the waiting helicopter near the hangar. Ryland struggled to keep up, the bulbous daypack on his right shoulder clumsily slapping against his side with each step.

Team leader Joshua Brins was standing beside the open cabin door of the unmarked black Bell 206. He shook his hands with Patterson then introduced him to the three other men before the director climbed inside.

Ryland paused next to Brins, catching his breath as he patted the operator on the shoulder, fixing his gaze on the man's face. "Good to meet you, Agent Brins. I hope you'll keep us all safe and get the job done."

"You can count on it, sir." Brins followed the stout man

into the bird then slid the door shut, giving the thumbs-up to the two pilots.

CHAPTER 31

AFTER GATHERING what information he could from Atley's laptop, Arlo Dewey drove back to his office on the east side of Blayne. He had instructed his two deputies to wait for the FBI agents who would be arriving in two hours and fill them in on the events at Mercer's cabin, the death of Atley, and the location where Crowe was last believed to be heading.

Dewey wasn't about to wait and play second fiddle to the incoming task force that would turn his town into a massive crime scene and restrict movement. Right now, his movement needed to be in the direction of Gould Canyon, where he figured Mercer was going.

He still wasn't sure who the hell Nick Mercer was, but he had seen that there were now three blips on Atley's satellite imagery, and that meant Angela was involved, whether willingly or not. And with this maniac Crowe on their trail, none of them would last until the Feds arrived.

Dewey unlocked the steel door to the back of his office then ran inside, grabbing his AR rifle, spare magazines and his backpack before snatching the keys off the wall for the county SAR vehicle.

He retraced his steps to the gravel parking lot, trotting to the Dodge Ram along the back fence. Dewey inspected the tie-downs attached to the ATV in the bed then got into the truck and sped out of the lot.

While it didn't show up on any maps, Dewey was familiar with an overgrown jeep trail known only to himself and a handful of old cowboys who used the gnarly route to herd cattle down to the San Juan River during drought years, when the waterholes on the mesa were bone dry. It was a nine-mile drive in his truck down a seasonally maintained dirt road, after which he'd need the ATV to negotiate three miles of rugged terrain along the old trail that terminated at the river. Once he was there, he planned to activate the personal location beacon in his pack whose satellite features would send his location to his deputies.

As he rushed along the blacktop heading west out of town, he hoped there would be enough time to intercept Mercer and Angela before Crowe's men got there.

CHAPTER 32

"THERE'S an obstruction of rocks about halfway down, but their tracks end there. Looks like they climbed through a small opening," said Ward, the bearded mercenary who had just returned from scouting the mineshaft.

Crowe walked to the narrow entrance of the tunnel, staring at the ground, then moved back towards the mouth that opened onto Black Canyon. "Well, shit. We're going to lose a lot of time if we go back the way we just came."

He waved the barrel of his AR towards the mineshaft. "Let's take that. At least we know for sure they went that way."

Ward went first, turning his headlamp back on and duck-walking through the tunnel. Crowe went next, followed by Hakim.

A few minutes later, they arrived at the rockpile. Ward removed his pack and slid it through the opening, followed by his rifle, then he began shimmying through the crevice.

There was a cool breeze wafting through the passage from the darkness, which Crowe figured was a good sign, since it meant that there was indeed another route out of here and that Mercer probably wasn't holed up inside somewhere waiting to snipe them.

He also knew that there were only a few hours of daylight left and that if Mercer was planning to get away on the San Juan River, he was running out of time.

Everything always boils down to how much sand is in the hourglass. We just need to get him and get the fuck out of here before the Feds or Dewey and his stooges arrive.

Crowe's attention shot back to the present.

The air filled with screams as Ward's legs thrashed in the opening.

Hakim rushed up alongside Crowe, both men tearing at the rocks around the top then pulling on the shrieking man's ankles. He slid down the rocks, a steel contraption clamped around his right forearm, which had splinters of bone jutting up.

The tunnel filled with Ward's howling as the man tried to peel off the trap, flinging his body against Hakim.

"Shit, he's going to bleed out. Hold him still so I can get that thing off, then I can put a tourniquet on," said Hakim, shuffling to the side as blood spurted from the mangled limb.

Crowe slid his left hand up over his right ear then turned his head slightly before raising his Glock and firing a single round into Ward's skull.

"Fuck. What the hell, Deke?" shouted Hakim as he backed up against the opposite wall.

"This is better for everyone here, especially him." He grabbed the dead man's vest, yanking him back from the rockpile then pointing the pistol towards the narrow opening as he nodded at Hakim to move.

"Time's a-wasting, lad. And time equals diamonds in our pockets. Now go!"

CHAPTER 33

AFTER THEIR JOG across the wind-scoured peninsula, Mercer, Angela and Luce arrived at the rim of Gould Canyon. The sand was blowing in full-force now, obliterating their tracks but also making it difficult to breathe given all the fine dust, pollen and debris in the air.

Scanning his normal route to the bottom, he felt his stomach coil in knots. The path down was choked with massive boulders that had cleaved off from the opposite side.

Shit. No!

He scrambled over to a cluster of small hackberry trees, squatting down as the woman and dog joined him. He studied the obliterated game trail at the bottom and the truck-sized boulders that would take hours of hazardous work to cross.

"Musta happened after the torrential rains we had last month," he said.

"Now what?" she said.

There were no other options. He had planned for every contingency except this. The hundred-year rainfall that had pounded the Four Corners last month had caused tremendous damage in the outlying communities, but he never thought it would completely cut off his escape route.

Mercer glanced around the mesa. *If we stay here, we'll be sniped by Crowe's guys in seconds, and we can't return to Black Canyon.*

He swung his head to the left, examining the vertical walls of Gould Canyon. During brief lulls in the savage winds, he heard a familiar hum.

He paused, adjusting the pack, staring towards the north.

Then he heard it again.

It was the sound of helicopter rotors. His eyes strained to pick out movement, and a black blip appeared in the brown haze as a chopper landed a half-mile north on a flat bench of sandstone.

A few minutes later, the rotors stopped, but no one exited.

Deke must have called in reinforcements.

Mercer didn't wait to see how many mercs would be sweeping along the mesa. He redoubled his efforts to get below. He tugged on Angela's sleeve.

"We need to get around this rockslide in order to make it to the river, so I hope you're not afraid to rappel?"

"Won't be my first time...occupational hazard."

"Good to hear, but it'll probably be your first time holding a dog."

"Uhm, yeah, I imagine so."

She and Luce followed him as he headed towards an immense pine tree hugging the edge of the canyon. Mercer tore open his pack, removing the climbing rope and the harness with the carabiner attached to the middle.

He handed Angela the MK12 then went about tying the

rope around the eighteen-inch base of the pine, securing it with a bowline. When he was done, Mercer leaned over towards Angela, offering to exchange the harness for his rifle.

He motioned for her to stand up then had her step into the harness, sliding it up into place and tightening it before running the rope through the carabiner and securing it back into the figure-8 knot already in place.

"I'll send your pack and mine down next, then I'll come after that."

She nodded then moved towards the edge. He removed a Petzl stop descender device from his pack, weaving the 10mm rope in and through the contraption, which would allow Angela to use the attached brake to control her downward speed.

Mercer glanced back in the direction where he'd seen the helicopter, which was now obscured in cascading waves of brown as the intensity of the storm picked up.

He gave Luce the command to come beside him and sit then picked her up, giving her a brief hug and kissing her on the head. He handed the dog to Angela then used several crisscross passes of 550 paracord under the woman's arms and around her waist to lash the dog as firmly to Angela's torso as possible.

He gave her a thumbs-up, hoping she was as skilled in the risky undertaking as she had suggested. Angela whispered something to Luce, who had buried her head in the woman's armpit.

Angela looked over her shoulder, taking baby steps to the edge then slowly easing them both over the rim while controlling the braking speed as they disappeared into the gorge.

Mercer returned to his pack, grabbing the MK12 then

squatting near the trees with his attention directed towards the mesa, which was slowly being erased as the wall of sand and debris moved towards Gould Canyon.

A few minutes later, he saw the rope go slack. He backpedaled to the rim, seeing Luce and Angela on a rock shelf forty feet below. She looked at him, giving a thumbs-up while Luce danced in circles around her legs.

Mercer hoisted up the rope, harness and descender, then he returned to the tree, grabbing their two packs. He ran the rope through the shoulder straps of both backpacks then tied off the end with a slippery bowline, which would be secure but allow for a speedy uncoupling for Angela once it arrived below.

He rechecked his external pouches and flap to make sure nothing would fall out then ran through the same check on Angela's pack. Mercer flipped open the top to cinch together the mouth of the main compartment, which had come undone, his eyes blinking hard at the faint outline of something standing out from the spare clothes.

He reached inside, pushing apart the other items, staring in bewilderment at a five-round rifle magazine with .308 caliber bullets.

CHAPTER 34

CROWE EMERGED from the vertical mineshaft, the sting of sand and debris whipping his face. He ducked back down for a second, putting on his sunglasses then pulling up the shemagh around his mouth and nose.

He wriggled free of the narrow opening, crawling along the ground to a fin-shaped slab of sandstone jutting out of the ground. There were a couple sets of faint boot tracks tucked next to the sandstone, which had provided some protection from the howling winds.

"Two, this is One, over," he said as his remaining men crawled up beside him. He made several more futile attempts to contact Atley then gave up, figuring something had happened at the cabin to compromise his position.

He switched channels, contacting Rohrbach's cyber crew. "Anything on Hendrix?"

"That whole area is just a big brown spot right now. The only thing I have is from about thirty minutes ago during a break in the storm...two people and a dog heading southwest towards a canyon about a mile from your location."

"Does that canyon end at the river?"

"Affirmative."

"What access points are along the rim?"

"Looks like only one route down on the east side, but it's filled with boulders. There is, however, a narrow trail along the beach at the mouth of the canyon where it meets the river on the west side. That probably doesn't help you much, but I show someone on an ATV moving towards the mouth of Gould Canyon."

Has to be Dewey. That inbred motherfucker.

Crowe felt a tap on his right shoulder. He glanced to where Hakim was pointing, catching intermittent glimpses of a black orb standing motionless in the cascading waves of sand scouring the mesa.

"Fuckin' A. It's about time," he said, sweeping his rifle towards the helicopter. "That's our ride out of here."

Hakim raised his binoculars again, scrutinizing the helicopter. "You sure? There are no markings on that bird. That's not one of ours."

"I got a message from one of my former contacts before we went into the tunnel. He's going to give us a ride out of here. Said he already worked out a deal with Rohrbach."

"And you trust this guy?"

"Hell yeah. He's the one who first introduced me to Edgar years ago."

Crowe stood up, preparing to make the sprint towards Gould Canyon.

CHAPTER 35

BRINS and his men donned their small backpacks then grabbed their AR-10s, each of them staring out the windows of the helicopter which felt like it was being assaulted by a small tornado.

He scanned the terrain to the south and east, the canyons and buttes obliterated by the coffee-colored silt that sandblasted the sides of the Bell 206.

"It looks like it might clear up shortly, but this is as far as we go for now," said the pilot as he turned off the engines.

"It doesn't matter," said Patterson, gazing at the red blip on his tablet, which showed satellite footage from his intel analyst back at Langley. "We're close enough. The subjects you're after are approximately 700 meters to the southwest of us. There are two of them...just be damn sure to remember which one has the kill order and which one is to be captured."

Patterson sat up, tapping on another tab then turning his device around to show his team the image of a redheaded woman. "This is an asset of mine. She was part of another phase of this operation, one which was about to yield results until Crowe and his thugs showed up. She will no doubt be in possession of knowledge that could be a threat to national security, so bring her and Mercer back here alive at all costs. Is that understood?"

The men all nodded. Brins lowered the wrap-around goggles on his head then pressed in closer to the side windows, watching another wave of sand rip across the mesa. He gave Ryland a sideways glance then gazed back at each of his men as he clutched the door handle. "Alright, fellas, let's go. We don't get paid to only work under blue skies."

CHAPTER 36

MERCER STUCK the rifle magazine back into Angela's pack, securing the top, then inspected the bowline again before lowering both packs over the rim.

As he fed the rope over the side, he thought back to the claustrophobic look on Angela's face when they entered the mineshaft, like it was the first time she'd even been inside a structure.

And later, her unfamiliarity with hantavirus, which was standard OSHA training for archeologists and mine inspectors. Though he didn't think it was unusual at the time, he recalled the heated conversation between Crowe and him on the radio earlier, and how all she seemed interested in afterwards was the location of the diamonds.

Then the way she held the MK12 a few minutes ago with her trigger finger properly indexed on the rifle body and her elbows tucked in like an experienced shooter.

His mind raced back to their first meeting in the coffee shop in Blayne in early August and their subsequent interactions, even leading up to their date a few days ago.

On each occasion, he had initiated contact.

She must have known my schedule somehow or my whereabouts. She made sure she was in the right place at the right time then led me to believe I was the one making the first move so she wouldn't arouse any suspicions about being interested in me.

Fuck.

He shook his head, reprimanding himself for not recognizing the fundamentals of acquiring assets and being a professional infiltrator.

With his lack of romantic opportunities in Blayne and his years of being emotionally isolated, he was the perfect mark for an alluring woman like Angela.

All she had to do was be aloof and provide enough opportunities to approach her to strike up a conversation and start things in motion.

So, is she with the Agency, coming to collect on their missing funds, or a freelancer who's just after the diamonds...and the bounty on my head?

He pried his eyes away from the woman below untying the packs. If Luce wasn't with her, Mercer would have thought of just leaving Angela behind, but he also knew that the path below was the only option for getting to the San Juan now.

He pulled up the slack rope, running it through the harness around his waist and legs, knowing he'd have to sort out what he was going to do with her fast.

But he was almost certain that would mean putting a bullet in the woman's head.

CHAPTER 37

ANGELA HUDDLED under the withered arms of a dead pinon pine tree with her arm around Luce, staring up at the cliff while awaiting Mercer's descent.

The blowing sand had slightly abated since she had entered the confines of the canyon, but the wind was now concentrated in these narrows, and her hearing was rendered useless, allowing her thoughts to close in on her.

Since she had gone on the run with Mercer following Crowe's appearance, she hadn't been able to get a message out on her SAT phone or cellphone to her superior.

Soon, she and Mercer would be at the river, and she figured either Mercer had arranged to be picked up in a small boat by someone or he had a canoe hidden somewhere.

Where they would end up after that was another mystery, but she hoped that it would result in her gaining the location of the diamonds that had caused her life to intersect with his and the good people of Blayne two months ago.

Angela had done her best to maintain an expression of

naiveté in the mineshaft earlier when Mercer was discussing what he'd done with the Agency's funds in Liberia, but the rest of his story and his interactions with Crowe had been a revelation.

Hendrix—or Mercer—wasn't the treasonous, corrupt agent that the CIA made him out to be.

She shook her head, wondering how her undercover mission here had turned into a chaotic mess whose outcome was still nebulous.

Since she had gone on her jog at dawn and checked her device for monitoring the GPS tracking chip she had put on Luce's collar, she knew the two had to be together along the rim of Black Canyon, which was unusual, but there had been no communication with her boss Patterson to alert her to any threats in the region.

After speaking with Dewey, she was convinced Mercer's cover was blown and that he was about to be snatched up by someone outside of the Agency. Later, heading to the rocky escarpment along Black Canyon, her fears were confirmed when she sighted an armed man through her rifle scope two hundred yards beyond Mercer's location by a rock spire.

The arrival of the SUV coincided with the armed man lining up Mercer in his rifle sights.

Her decision to pull the trigger on the distant shooter took form when Mercer began sniping Crowe's guys. As soon as she saw Mercer and Luce heading towards the fissure, she decided that ditching her rifle and joining them was the only option to help keep him from being captured or killed by Crowe.

Angela sighed, trying to convince herself that an Agency team was in that black helicopter above the rim, but it seemed like her boss Patterson would have already notified her, making her wonder who the new players were.

Crowe with more of his goons, or is that an FBI tac-team? Or is the Agency itself coming to torch all of us to cover their tracks?

Living with turmoil and uncertainty had always felt like a normal state of mind for Angela, who had bounced around the foster care system most of her adolescence then been recruited out of college into the Agency.

Deep cover work allowed her to forge a new identity and start with a clean slate, wearing elaborately knit personalities that she could pull down over the scars on her soul, which was far easier than living with what life had previously provided.

But her assignments had involved infiltrating multiple criminal networks in Latin America, where her Agency-trained Spanish language skills had come to fruition.

Then came Blayne and her cover story. Patterson arranged for her to spend a week with a retired Agency colleague who had grown up in the mines in West Virginia. It laid the foundation for understanding the unique terminology, mindset and some of the specialized skills needed to foster her new identity while Patterson created the company façade behind Palladium Industries.

But it was Blayne itself which surprised her. The sleepy town and caring people showed her what a community could be like. For the first time, she found herself completely absorbed by her new identity, glancing through real estate brochures on trips to Moab and seeing the potential for a life beyond undercover work which she was more than ready to have come to an end.

She pulled Luce closer, staring into the soulful eyes of the trusting dog. "And you, sweet girl, I don't know what we're going to do with you yet, but I promise I'll always protect you.

As she watched Mercer rappel down, she hoped she

could say the same thing about the man she'd come to know...or thought she knew. His identities and stories blurred in her thinking, but her gut told her that Patterson had only provided morsels of information to help keep her emotions out of the equation.

Maybe Patterson knows me better than I thought.

Angela seethed out an exhale, silently cussing the schizophrenic double life and endless lies associated with deep cover work. She wondered how many more years of this job she could take and what would be left of her by the end.

CHAPTER 38

NEIL PATTERSON GAZED past the pilot on the left, seeing a sliver of blue sky emerging in the distance as the winds eased slightly. The waves of sand had ceased, and the helicopter was no longer swaying from the storm.

He fixed his attention back on Ryland, who was nervously tapping on his phone then cursing at the lack of reception.

The portly man swiveled around towards the two pilots, seeing them scanning the navigational equipment. "You guys having any interference with your comms?"

"No, sir," said the copilot on the right.

"It's just your device," said Patterson. "You remember my analyst Lynn Vogel...I had her deactivate it."

"What? Why?"

"You know, I recruited Joshua Brins personally, as I do all of my teams. When Vogel told me she intercepted a phone message sent from my jet to the Whitman Airfield in Salt Lake, I was a little surprised, so I got a hold of a colleague at the NSA and had them track down that call."

Ryland squirmed back, licking his lips. "You're a paranoid son of a bitch, Neil. You always were."

He chuckled. "And that's a liability in this business?" Patterson waved his hand towards the desert, seeing the storm clouds continuing to push north while the skies overhead returned to their cobalt hue. "Let's go for a walk, Garrett."

Rylan clasped his hands, pushing back into his seat.

"Now! Open the door and get out," said Patterson, who was moving towards the case officer.

Ryland leaned on the handle, twisting it up then shoving the door outward. A trickle of grit cascaded down off the top edge onto his back as he lowered himself onto the slickrock. Patterson followed behind, slamming the door then removing a Ruger LC9 pistol from his jacket.

The director thrust his chin towards the canyon beyond the rear of the helicopter as he motioned with the pistol. Ryland's face drained of color as he turned and walked in front of Patterson as the two men headed towards Gould Canyon, sixty-feet in the distance.

Ryland paused a few feet from the rim, staring down at the sheer walls. "You expect me to jump...is that it?"

"You know, Garret, we're here right now because of you. Because of your greedy fucking paws. You are the leak in my division at Langley. I always suspected there was a connection between you and the Rohrbachs, given how Crowe mysteriously joined their ranks then somehow managed to escape the kill squad I put you in charge of in Sierra Leone."

Ryland glanced back at the helo then along the rim where Brins and his team had disappeared. "This is bullshit. It was that guy of yours, Hendrix. Why do you think there's a burn notice out on him?"

"I actually signed off on that burn notice but delayed pushing it through for forty-eight hours to help him avoid being gunned down by the Agency in the streets of Guinea. His only crime was doing the right thing in helping all those people escape the carnage in their own country...carnage that began when you recruited Crowe into Rohrbach's army."

Patterson leveled the Ruger at Ryland's chest. "And before you think Brins is going to come to your rescue, you should know that he called me immediately after you spoke with him about lining his bank account if he'd put a bullet in my head. That lad knows what honor and integrity are, just as Hendrix did. Unlike you, you piece of shit."

Ryland's lips quivered. "My father was a lawyer at the Agency. There's no way any of this is going to hold up, you bastard."

"You really think he or the Agency is going to let news of your fucking treason get out in the open?"

Patterson quickly raised the pistol higher and off to the left of Ryland's head then squeezed off a single round that strafed the air beside the man's ear. Ryland careened to the side, wincing as he perilously teetered on the edge of the canyon, his pear-shaped body wobbling as his eyes widened. He shrieked, thrusting a hand towards Patterson then tumbled over, striking a rock slab on the way down before careening along the boulders like a shattered coconut.

The director knelt down, retrieving the brass casing then sliding it into his coat pocket along with the pistol. He returned to the helicopter, yanking open the door then returning to his seat.

The pilots looked back at him then out towards the canyon. "Is Mr. Ryland alright?" said the lead pilot.

"Tragically, he lost his footing."

The two pilots gave each other sideways glances, gazing out the side window towards the open maw of Black Canyon, then slowly swiveled back around in their seats, their postures rigid.

Patterson heard his earpiece crackle as Brins shouted amidst the sound of gunfire.

When he was done speaking to his agent, Patterson leaned in towards the pilots. "Brins' team is down. They were ambushed at the rim by shooters in the canyon. I can only assume that it was Crowe and his guys."

He slid back into the seat, buckling up. "Brins made it below before it all went to hell, so if you gentlemen deem that this weather is suitable enough to fly, I need you to take us down to the mouth of Black Canyon pronto."

CHAPTER 39

MERCER LED the way to the river, feeling like he had a bullseye on his back with Angela behind him.

The last half-mile of the canyon widened considerably as they neared the end, the sandy substrate turning into gravel then football-sized rocks as it terminated at the San Juan.

Luce ran ahead, splashing in the water and lapping up the cool fluid as Mercer climbed up a short, rocky incline on the left, stopping at a narrow shelf before an overhang.

Like he had before in the mineshaft, he went about using a buried mallet and chisel to remove the concealed cache in a recess in the rock face.

When he was done extracting the dufflebag inside containing a rolled-up inflatable kayak, he set it aside then retrieved a waterproof case from his backpack, pulling out a SAT phone and dialing the only pre-listed number.

On the fourth ring, the comforting voice of a familiar man responded.

"It's me," said Mercer. "Remember that I said there

would come a time when I need you to pick me up at the rendezvous site?"

"When?" the man said.

"Should be two hours, maybe three?"

"That's about how long it will take me to drive out there."

"Thanks, brother. See you soon."

He hung up, returning the device to its case.

"Eddie Peshlakai?" shouted Angela from below.

Mercer swiveled his head, giving her an irritated glance. He chided himself for sharing too much of his life with her over the past two months.

He didn't respond but motioned for Angela to come up.

"I need some help inflating this little boat," he said, tossing her the hand-pump. As soon as it landed in her hands, he rushed forward, slamming her back into the wall then jamming the barrel of his Glock against her chin.

"Give me one good reason, besides upsetting my dog, why I shouldn't end you right here."

"What the hell are you doing?" She didn't resist, leaning back into the sandstone.

He lifted her shirt a few inches, feeling around her back then removing a .380 Kahr pistol from her belt.

Mercer stepped back. "Here's how this is going to work, Angela Owens. I'm going to ask some questions while you inflate this kayak. If at any time I sense you are giving me a line of bullshit or if you try to make a move at me, you get a hollowpoint in that pretty head of yours."

He kicked the hand-pump towards her. Angela bit her lip, narrowing her eyes, then knelt down, following through on his demands.

Mercer stepped to the side, standing next to his rifle

leaning against the dufflebag, and alternated between watching Angela and scanning the canyon to the north.

"To answer your first question," she said, "you shouldn't 'end me' because I saved your fucking life earlier today when I took out that lone merc who was on your tail."

He raised an eyebrow. "That explains the mag I found in your pack. But not the why."

"My boss's intel wiz at Langley located you after your passports were discovered by INTERPOL last spring. I was brought in and instructed to gain your trust, making sure you stayed put while word of your location was leaked to Rohrbach and Crowe. All I was told was that Rohrbach had a bounty on your head for the diamonds you stole in Africa."

"First off, I only liberated those diamonds from Rohrbach after he stole them. Those stones and their riches belong to the people of Liberia, not me, or a diamond broker, or the Agency. And when the time is right, those funds will be delivered to the country where they were first discovered."

She lowered her head, continuing to work the pump. "Look, I didn't know about your past in Liberia. All I knew was that you were listed as a rogue agent who had stolen Agency funds before going dark."

He ground a pebble into the dirt with the tip of his boot. "And some rare fucking diamonds that could set you up for life, Angie...or whatever the fuck your name is."

"You should talk, *Nick*.

She turned away, staring out towards the canyon. "The file that my boss provided indicated that I was just supposed to keep an eye on you, and if you discovered your cover was blown, to follow you after you fled Blayne." Angela glanced down at Luce by the water. "I knew you'd be too hard to get a tracker on, but there was someone else who never left your side."

Mercer's face grew taut. "You're kidding. Tell me you didn't jab my dog with a GPS device?"

"You only had one soft spot. She was the way into your life. Sorry."

Mercer whistled, calling Luce back from the beach, disturbed that the tentacles of his past had infiltrated everything in Blayne that was precious to him.

"So what was your end game? Get the diamonds then put a bullet in my head while I slept? Or does Langley have its claws so deep into your back that you're incapable of determining where the line in the sand is at any longer?"

Angela flicked her head towards him. "I guess none of that matters anymore, since my future appears to be in your hands. So, what are *you* going to do if you make it out of here alive...shoot me in my sleep one day, or just kill me in this canyon?"

"I haven't decided yet." He removed the two-piece plastic-and-aluminum paddle from the dufflebag, connecting the two sections.

"So, who instructed you to embed yourself in Blayne and my life?"

She paused, blowing a strand of red hair off her nose. "My superior is Neil Patterson, Director of Field Operations at Langley."

Mercer emitted a faint grin. "Patterson...that slippery dog." He patted Luce on the neck. "No offense to you, girl." Mercer continued, "I'm almost certain that Patterson was the guy who notified me of the burn notice and told me to get out of Guinea. So, he did all of this just to lure in Rohrbach and Crowe... That's a pretty risky move, running an op like this on U.S. soil. But I can see why he em-*bed*-ded you in my life...excuse the pun."

"That last part wasn't the job." She leaned back on her heels, the ten-foot kayak fully inflated.

He waved the pistol towards her as she continued talking.

"Patterson knew there was a leak in his division at Langley and suspected it all went back to whatever happened in Liberia. When I heard you and Crowe talking on the radio earlier, I realized that Crowe was connected but that there had to be another player involved. That must be who Patterson was trying to root out, only he needed you as bait to lure in Crowe by leaking your blown passports."

"And you were my bait...nice job, Angela. You're a helluva operator and have quite a career ahead of you."

"Look, when we were together the other night...that wasn't pre-planned as part of my mission here. It was a first for me in undercover work, and I really wanted to be with you."

He waved a hand. "Yay, I'm so glad I could help activate your humanity software."

"Fuck you, Nick. Like you never deceived anyone in your job with the Agency. I know you sure had all the good people of Blayne fooled. Even Dewey...he's the only good one out of us all."

"You're sure right about that last part."

Mercer flicked his head towards the cluster of willows across the drainage, but he wasn't in time to see the shooter.

The flesh on his right bicep tore open as the canyon walls echoed with the sound of a single gunshot.

He tumbled back, dropping his pistol and rolling down the slope towards the river.

CHAPTER 40

BRINS HAD JUST WATCHED two of his men die on the rim after snipers picked them off, followed by his other agent, whose limp body was still dangling from the rope halfway down the rim.

It had been a quick, well-executed attack, but now he was alone at the bottom of the canyon. He forced down the anguish of losing his team, his friends, and focused on his surroundings. There would be time for mourning later.

He'd seen one of the shooters trotting south, but he figured the other sniper was nestled in the clusters of boulders to the right. Brins removed his ballcap, placing it on his pack beside the sandstone spire where he was concealed, then he crept to the opposite side, studying the nearest boulder through the Swarovski scope on his AR-10.

A second later, he saw a faint glimmer of movement along the cliff face. A bearded man darted between boulders, but there wasn't enough time for Brins to react.

Then he saw it again. The gap between the rocks too slim to afford a shot.

Brins focused on the terrain ahead, figuring that the

sniper had only stayed long enough to provide cover so his partner could head south.

You guys are on a tight timeline, aren't you, you bastards? That means you think your ride is inbound.

Brins stood up, leaning his left shoulder against the rock spire and focusing on the next logical place where the shooter would emerge.

He paced his breathing, knowing there would only be a microsecond to react.

Brins slid his finger down on the trigger, steadying his sights in line with the direction of travel that the man would have to pass through to get to the next boulder, which was spaced a little further apart.

A flash of black amidst the tawny rocks.

He squeezed off a single round.

The figure stumbled then slowed, finally collapsing to his knees as red leaked from his ribcage. Brins sent another round through the skull, watching his enemy fall to the ground.

CHAPTER 41

THE PAIN in Mercer's arm was excruciating, and he choked down the urge to vomit as he turned onto his left side, glancing at the finger-wide furrow of bloody pulp where a bullet had grazed his right bicep.

He searched for his pistol and Angie's Kahr, but they were nowhere in sight. Mercer removed the shemagh around his neck, using it as an improvised bandage. He figured Crowe's shot had been intentionally placed so he didn't bleed out.

He crabbed his way back around the mouth of the canyon, figuring Crowe was still in the willows searching for him. That only one shot had been fired was a relief, and he figured that Angela had dove for cover with Luce in tow.

He was pissed at himself for being so immersed in hearing her side of the story that he failed to detect the shooter.

Maybe I am rusty as hell.

He thought about what she'd said and the fact that she had already saved his life once today by taking out one of Crowe's mercs. It didn't help his internal argument that Luce liked the woman, and he was beginning to question the dog's soundness.

Mercer angled his head out from the rocks, seeing the edge of the willow grove but not detecting any movement. He was about to crawl up the slope to retrieve his MK12 when he heard the crunching of sand behind him.

He turned, seeing Dewey squat-walking towards him with his rifle pointed at his chest.

"Damn, Arlo, am I ever glad to see you."

"Shut up, you lyin' piece of shit. I oughta drag your ass into the river and let you drown."

Mercer grit his teeth. "Guess I had that coming. Does that mean you're here to arrest me or to help me take down Crowe?"

"At least one of those for sure. We'll see about the other depending on the next words that come out of your damn mouth."

"In all the time I've known you, I've only ever heard you cuss one time."

"Yeah, well, right now seems like a good time to change my ways."

Mercer returned his gaze towards the willows, wondering what Crowe was planning.

"Did you kill those people in Liberia, Nick? Is that even your real name?"

"I can shake my head til I'm dizzy, but you're a good judge of character, Arlo. I think you know I didn't."

"I saw the laptop that belonged to one of Crowe's guys... heard some mention of stolen diamonds that you had. Is that what this is all about?"

Mercer rolled his eyes up at the cliffs, hoping he wouldn't have to do another recap on the event in Liberia that had brought near-destruction to his doorstep.

"That's a big part of this. That and the fact I used to work for the CIA for years. I used the Agency's money to help get a bunch of families to safety after Crowe decided to torch the Liberian countryside so his boss could control the diamond mines." Mercer glanced back towards the bottom of the canyon, searching for movement.

He could tell Arlo was processing the information along with the events of the past twenty-four hours. Mercer wished he could sit down and explain the whole thing and the deception behind his life in Blayne, but daylight wasn't on his side, and he had to get on the river soon or blow his timeline for making it to Eddie.

"Look, Arlo, I know I spun a whole lotta bullshit to you over the years about my past, and you're probably questioning everything about our friendship, but right now, I need you to trust your instincts and let me just finish what I started...let me get on the river and away from here. This is about more than you and me and Angela. Generations of people in West Africa will be affected by the outcome of what happens here right now if I don't put an end to this."

Dewey extended his pistol hand, narrowing his eyes as he focused on the willows in the distance. "'The sheriff who couldn't be corrupted'...I reckon you've heard that before. Everyone has who meets me."

"I know." Mercer kept his gaze focused on the canyon.

"Then you probably know how that story ends too."

"You upheld the law and turned in your own boss. I do know. I also know that two people's lives were affected in ways you could never have imagined."

"I did the right thing, and a mother and daughter suffered the ultimate consequences. Good people who should have gone on to better lives, if only I hadn't stepped forward."

Mercer scrunched his eyebrows together, thinking back on his past actions and recent events with Angela. "Part of doing the right thing is knowing you might risk everything, even the fate of the people around you. What happened, Arlo, wasn't a reflection on you but on the sheriff who made all those decisions leading up to that tragic event. What happened to the wife and daughter wasn't your fault."

Dewey gave him a surprised look. "You've known all this time?"

"Believe me when I say, I've seen the horrors that people can inflict on others. Coming here, getting to know you and the other people in Blayne...you restored my faith in humanity, my friend."

Mercer glanced at the sunlight slipping from the canyon walls then waved out to the river. "What's it going to be, Arlo? Whatever you decide, I'll live with it, but let me take down Crowe first."

Dewey looked at the silty waters of the San Juan then gave Mercer a piercing stare. "You got a lifejacket for Luce, or you want her to stay here with me?"

"She's going to be better equipped than I am." He extended his hand, glancing down at his service pistol.

Dewey bit his lower lip then removed his Sig 226, handing it over.

"What's your plan?" said the sheriff.

"Fill Crowe with hollowpoints."

"Seems pretty straightforward."

Mercer sat up, secreting his back against the cliff wall then working his way slowly around the mouth of the canyon. When he could see the willow grove, he raised up the pistol, grimacing from the pain in his arm but focusing the front sight on the most likely place he would hide as a shooter.

"He's still in there somewhere, waiting to nail one of us or waiting for his guys to reach our location."

"What do you want me to do?" said the sheriff as he moved up along Mercer's right side.

Before Nick could react to Dewey's exposure, another shot rang out. He heard a thump behind him but immediately fired a few rounds into the willow thicket where he'd seen the muzzle blast.

Then he dropped down, sliding back towards Dewey, who was lying on his back. The man's right pectoral near the shoulder was pumping out blood.

"No!" Mercer tore off his shirt, wadding it up and placing it over Dewey's wound.

"This wasn't the damn plan, Arlo."

Angela crawled up beside him with Luce on her heels. The dog trotted around Dewey, licking his cheek as the man groaned in pain.

"What happened? What the hell's he even doing out here?" snapped Angela.

"Did you see if the shooter is down?"

"Not sure."

"Get the trauma kit from my backpack. Hurry."

She crept back around the base of the rock ledge, returning a few minutes later. He tore the trauma kit from her hands then broke out an Israeli bandage, placing it over the bullet wound. Next, he removed a small morphine injectable, jabbing it into Dewey's right arm.

Angela had already picked up the sheriff's AR and was sweeping the willow grove while Mercer continued his combat-medic duties.

"His breathing isn't wheezy, so his lung must not have collapsed, which is good, but we'll need to get him to a hospital."

"Thought you needed to get on the river?" she said.

"I'm not leaving him here to die."

"Even if it means missing your window for escape?"

"Would you shut up already?"

"If you'll shut up about me staying over at your cabin the other night as part of my job description."

When he'd finished tending to Dewey, he glanced along the canyon floor then out towards the thick clumps of willows on the opposite side where the shooter was situated.

He gave Luce the hand command to stay then glanced at Angela. "Take up a position near the ledge here. I'm going to make my way along the boulders parallel to the river. Wait for my hand signal then lay down some gunfire on that grove."

She nodded, clutching the AR and doing a chamber check then flicking off the safety. While she moved into position beside an angled wedge of sandstone, Mercer crouch-trotted to the first boulder. There were enough clumps of tamarisk and shrubs in between the rocks to cloak his passage, but he still broke up the cadence of his bounds to prevent betraying his passage.

Thirty yards later, he crouched against the last boulder in the middle of the canyon just before it met the San Juan. He lay flat, peering around the right side, his face concealed in the low grass jutting from the base of the immense rock. He had a clear shot of the willows but still no sign of his quarry.

Mercer leaned back until he could see Angela then gave a thumbs-up, quickly swiveling back to his shooting position.

A cacophony of gunshots rang out from her location. Then he saw the muzzle flash in the willows as return fire ensued. It was low. A foot off the ground.

Mercer steadied the sights on his Sig, aiming for where he thought the torso was located, then squeezed off five shots in rapid succession. Immediately, he leaned back, thrusting his fist up towards Angela to stop shooting.

Then he sprang up, darting towards the back of the willow grove and arcing in towards his target. A groaning sound emanated from the brush where Crowe was lying, crimson leaking from the left armpit and upper ribcage above his vest.

Mercer rushed forward, kicking away the man's rifle. Crowe sluggishly turned on his side, removing a pistol, but Mercer sent a vicious heel stomp into the man's wrist, pinning it against the ground.

"You're not gonna let me go down without a good fight?" Crowe chuckled, coughing out some blood.

Mercer grabbed the man's pistol, tucking it into his belt-line, then stepped back. "Was it all worth it, Deke? Coming here to die in this canyon?"

"You know better than me that none of us are gonna make it to retirement. If I could have gotten those diamonds, at least it would have been a fun ride to the edge of the cliff." He winced, leaning to his side as he clasped his hand around his wound. "Besides, I been hurt worse than this and bounced back...you know me, partner."

"You stopped being my partner, my friend, five years ago when you unleashed a world of suffering upon the people we were sent to help."

Crowe tried to sit up. "Go ahead then, put one between my eyes and get it over with already."

Mercer removed his knife, leaning over Crowe. "And give you a quick ride out of here?" His blade hand shot down, the tip deftly slicing along Crowe's right thigh, severing the femoral.

Crowe's eyes widened, his mouth hanging open as he watched the bright red blood throbbing out as his hands frantically pressed on the spurting wound. He shrieked, pawing at his leg as the ground turned crimson. Then he fell back, his face ashen. "I'll see you again, old friend. I'll see you..."

Thirty seconds later, the flies had already gathered on the dead man's face and glassy eyes. Mercer stepped back, sucking in a deep breath. He stared down at his bloody hands, wondering how much was from him, Crowe and Dewey, making him wish this was all over.

But he still had to get help for the sheriff and somehow get on the river before the Feds showed up.

He dragged his blade across some grass then resheathed it, heading back towards Angela. Luce greeted him affectionately, hopping at his feet as he knelt down and petted her while looking over at Dewey.

"The morphine is really kicking in. He's going to be loopy soon." Angela put her hand on Mercer's shoulder. "You alright?"

He glanced at the willows then back to the sheriff. "Yeah, but we need to get Arlo out of here. He must have come in on his ATV, which is probably just about a quarter-mile down from here along a small pullout, from what I recall of the area."

"I'll take care of him," she said. "He mumbled something about using his personal location beacon to notify his deputies of his location, so they're most likely gonna be on their way here soon."

A second later, the sand was beginning to swirl around them as the noise of rotors echoed off the canyon walls. Mercer leaned back, seeing a black helicopter descending then landing on the beach.

He gave Luce the command to stay, and the dog lay down beside Arlo, whose wincing had reduced to low groans.

"Better find some cover and get ready to send some more hate downrange," he yelled at Angela.

The rotors came to a standstill, and she immediately lowered her weapon after seeing Patterson emerge. The copilot stepped out next, keeping his pistol at a low-ready as he walked beside the director.

Patterson moved past the willows then along the array of boulders, pausing next to the yellow kayak before standing a few feet from the trio of survivors. "I figured I would just follow the trail of bodies you left behind and I'd find you at the end," he said, staring at Mercer.

Nick lowered his pistol then stood up to face his former training officer. "And you look older than I remember...sir."

Patterson chuckled, turning around as they all watched Brins coming down the middle of the canyon, moving towards the willow grove to inspect the dead body. The man fired three rounds into Crowe's face before making his way over to the group.

Mercer studied the younger agent's tan face. "You look familiar. Have we met before?"

"Algeria. Five, maybe six years ago."

"Six," said Mercer. "Glad you're still kickin' around."

"Me too." Brins thrust his thumb up canyon. "My men weren't so lucky. All three of them...they..." He shook his head, glancing back at the dead man in the grove.

"I'm sorry," said Mercer. He thought of the awful toll that clandestine work had on its agents and anyone connected to them. He was tired of the lies, the constant threat assessments of the people around him, and the need for evasion plans for every scenario in his daily life.

He just wanted to sit on his back porch again and watch the stars at night. Now, his fate would be decided by the man before him.

Patterson tapped his earpiece, speaking to someone for a few minutes before turning around to the group. "My analyst has indicated that the FBI will be arriving in Blayne within minutes, it seems." He nodded towards Dewey. "The good news is that there's a sheriff's vehicle heading to this location in about twenty minutes."

He moved closer to Mercer and Angela. "And we have some things to discuss before we can all depart these shores."

CHAPTER 42

MERCER STOOD in the shade of a cottonwood tree near his kayak while Patterson recounted the events that had unfolded during the early conception of his plans involving Crowe and Ryland along with Angela's pivotal role in its completion. While they spoke, Brins tended to Dewey, keeping the man hydrated and cool.

"Once your passports were discovered at Hassan's place by INTERPOL last spring, the Deputy Director of the CIA agreed with me that you could be used to lure in Rohrbach and Crowe, which would help me flush out the mole in our own ranks. We knew this would also take time, so I was instructed to use my own resources and personnel to keep tabs on you so you didn't disappear again. That's where Angela came in."

"So she was only known to you and your immediate staff?" said Mercer as he glanced at the redhead, who wore a look of defiance.

"Yes. She had been doing deep cover work for several years but wanted out. We agreed that after this assignment, she could choose whether to continue in another division or opt out of the Agency altogether."

Patterson moved closer. "So, my boy, that just leaves one nagging thorn in both of our sides...one that will only fester and continue to create more problems over time."

"Rohrbach."

Patterson nodded. "His influence in African politics has become too significant to U.S. interests in the region, not to mention the multiple civil wars he's been responsible for fueling." The director folded his arms, glancing up at a raven. "What would you say if I could make your burn notice disappear?"

Mercer rubbed his chin. "*If* I eliminate Rohrbach? Is that it?"

The older man grinned. "After what unfolded here during these past forty-eight hours, I'd say you haven't lost your edge. Plus, with Crowe and his senior cadre out of the way that leaves Rohrbach's company vulnerable."

"I'd also say that a man needs the resources to pull off something on that scale."

He glanced beyond Mercer, watching Angela as she walked away to trade places with Brins. "She knows how to reach me. I'll be waiting for your call. But just keep in mind that this offer has an expiration date."

He and Patterson exchanged handshakes, and Mercer leaned closer. "Just between us, did you send me that message in Guinea about the burn notice?"

"You did call me old earlier, and my memory isn't what it once was." Patterson turned and walked away.

Mercer watched him walk back to the helicopter. The old man got on board, followed by Brins, who leaned out, staring at Mercer for a second then nodding before sliding the door closed.

Nick retraced his steps back to the boat, seeing he only just had enough daylight left to make it to the rendezvous point with Eddie Peshlakai.

He knelt down beside Dewey and Angela. "Your deputies will be here soon, and the Feds will be with them, Arlo, so I need to get a move on it."

"My guys are going to be glad I'm out of the office for a few days." Dewey coughed then grimaced from the effort.

"More like a few weeks, I'd say," replied Mercer. He reached down and grabbed the sheriff's hand. "You are what is best in a man, my friend. I will miss you."

Dewey fought to keep his eyes open as the morphine continued to course through his body. "Wherever you end up after this, just make sure it's not in another small town. Not every sheriff is as hospitable as me."

"I will remember that." He patted the man on the side then motioned for Angela to follow him to the kayak.

"I know we're on rather new, if not entirely firm, ground, but I need to ask you for a favor."

She folded her arms. "Uhm, alright. I think."

He whistled, calling over Luce, then he leaned down and hugged the dog. "This time, I need you to stay put here with Ms. Angela, you little brat. She's going to watch over you until we meet up again."

"That I can do," the woman replied. "But 'Miss Angela,' really?"

He stood up, extending his hand. "Maybe one day, you'll tell me your real name."

She thrust her chin towards the river. "You better be on your way, don't you think?"

He glanced back at Dewey then at Luce before letting his eyes drift north along Gould Canyon towards the direction of his cabin one last time.

Mercer grabbed the end of the kayak and slid it into the water, checking the lashings on his backpack then hopping on and grabbing the paddle, letting his good arm take the brunt of the effort as he slipped into the main current.

The silty river quickly carried him west through a deepening gorge of sandstone cliffs and along the undulating contours of the San Juan.

And in eleven miles, he'd reach the designated takeout, his days as Nick Mercer coming to an end.

CHAPTER 43

Five Weeks Later

Langley, Virginia

Neil Patterson was sitting in his office, going over his budget for the following fiscal year, when he looked up at the three TV monitors on the wall.

He saw the headline at the bottom of the CNN broadcast announcing the death of billionaire Edgar Rohrbach and his board of directors, who had perished on the company yacht near the Virgin Islands after a fuel leak caused an explosion.

Patterson's pulse quickened. He grabbed the remote, unmuting the coverage on the ABC channel as he stared intently at the image of floating debris around where the vessel was last seen.

After glancing through the different broadcasts, which

all amounted to the same information, he muted the consoles.

Damn, he killed them all.

Patterson got up from his chair, walking to the window and gazing at the pedestrian traffic in the courtyard below, then out to a row of cumulus clouds in the distance. He let out a long exhale. After a few minutes, he returned to his desk, seeing an incoming call from a familiar number.

"How is your day going, sir?" said Mercer.

"Better than expected, actually. You were thorough...*extremely* thorough, I might add."

"Defanging the entire snake seemed like the most prudent move."

"I imagine so."

"So the agreement you and the director made will be honored?"

"Yes, your burn notice will be officially rescinded after I hang up."

"I'm curious, but what happened to Sheriff Dewey after all the smoke cleared in Blayne once the Feds wrapped up their investigation?"

"My understanding is that the FBI's sole focus was on Crowe and his crew, since they were responsible for the deaths of two of their agents. Dewey recovered from his wound, but that's all I know."

Patterson heard an audible sigh. A long silence followed, then the director spoke again. "Any immediate plans?"

"Well, I've really taken to the Caribbean lately, and there are a lot of tropical islands in these parts that I'd like to explore."

"I could see that being fulfilling...for a few months. But a guy like you always needs to be racing down the trail with his back on fire, not resigning to the life of a beach bum."

"A beach bum is an underrated profession and requires its own set of survival know-how."

"Nate, I've been in this business a long time and have seen my share of agents come and go, but you're one of the few with a unique blend of skills, instincts and operational experience, all of which have allowed you to make it this far."

"With all that sweet talk, I sense another job coming. Except I'm done after this."

"I always have an occasional need for a lone operator for various assignments...just keep it in mind for when you grow weary of sipping rum from your hammock."

"Gracias. I've got your number, but don't expect a call in the near future, or maybe ever."

"Take care, my boy."

"Likewise...and sir, thank you for looking out for me now...and five years ago."

Patterson heard the phone go silent then placed it on the desk. He sat down, rubbing the sides of his neck and letting his shoulders slouch.

For a few minutes, his mind was adrift, reflecting back on Hendrix, Liberia, Utah and the allure of dropping everything to sail off into the sunset. He sighed, sitting forward, placing his budget papers back in the folder and locking them in his desk then retrieving a bottle of brandy from the side drawer on his right.

Patterson poured half a glass, lifting it towards the news monitors, thinking the world would be a better place...for at least a few weeks more.

CHAPTER 44

ONE WEEK Later

TULUM, Mexico

BETH SULLIVAN LEANED OVER, grabbing the stick and tossing it into the tropical waters again. She watched the dog bolt for it as it had the last thirty times since she stepped off the porch of her bungalow.

She watched the mutt swim with childlike eagerness and retrieve its treasure then swim back to shore.

Beth grabbed the stick, flinging it once more into the bay.

When the dog returned this time, it paused on the beach, staring off to the left. It remained still for a long while then a tremor of movement overtook its body, its tail wagging with great gusto as it watched a barefoot man approaching.

Luce dropped the stick, bolting towards the figure.

Beth folded her arms, smiling at the frolicking dog, who was jumping at the man's face, licking his chin and then rolling on her back as he rubbed her belly.

"She's not up for adoption, in case you're wondering," said Beth as she moved closer.

The man stood up, his teeth accentuated by his thick beard. "Well, they say that dogs choose their people and not the other way around, though she sure seems at home with you."

"Don't worry, she's had that far-off look in her eyes every morning, staring out the patio door for her old hiking buddy."

He rubbed the pink scar on his right arm. "I can do without any more winding trails for a while."

"Speaking of winding trails, I read online yesterday that there's a series of new clinics and free aid stations being proposed in Liberia and Guinea after an anonymous donation of forty million dollars poured into the medical communities over there."

"That so?" He looked off to the horizon for a long while. "Well, those sure seem like places that could use a change of luck."

"And how's your luck going these days?"

He gave an easy grin, thrusting his chin towards the dock. "Down easy street, I'm hoping. I just got a new lease on life and a new sailboat."

She canted her head. "A boat, really? I kinda took you for a desert guy."

He pointed to the barren mountains in the distance. "I think I'm done with that world. Having a sailboat means a different view each week. Plus, there's not much fishing to be had in the desert."

"So are you thinking that a nomadic life is the way to go?"

He removed his sunglasses. "Lately, I'm thinking that a fresh start would be good."

She stepped closer, placing her hand on his bearded cheek. "A fresh start...I like that."

He extended his hand. "My name's Nate...Nate Hendrix."

"Beth."

His smile continued to grow. "Nice to meet you, Beth."

AFTERWORD

The high-desert region of Utah depicted in this book contains millions of untrammeled acres of prehistoric ruins, rock art, snow-capped mountains and miles of serpentine canyons. The names of the latter have all been changed in this story, but glance at a map of the Bears Ears National Monument and you will get a glimpse of this amazingly diverse and captivating area.

For many years, I taught extended survival courses for the military and general public in this slickrock wilderness, traversing its rugged terrain and marveling at its vistas. It is truly my favorite place on Earth and an ecosystem that has no equal.

Thanks for reading this book and coming along for the ride!

MORE ADVENTURES TO COME

Stay tuned for future books in the series. Join my email list at JTSawyer.com and you can grab a FREE military thriller short story, *Lethal Conduct*. Nate Hendrix also makes an appearance in *HAVOC,* Volume 5 in the *Search and Destroy Series.*

Stay updated with current happenings on my Facebook page, JTSawyerBooks.

Lastly, as an Indie writer, your feedback is critical to refining my craft. If you wouldn't mind posting a review on Amazon, I'd be grateful! Reviews make a world of difference in the life of a writer and help direct other readers to our works.

MORE ADVENTURES TO COME

ADDITIONAL TITLES BY JT SAWYER

Dead In Their Tracks: The Mitch Kearns Combat Tracker Series, Volumes 1–12

Meet Mitch Kearns, a former Special Forces Combat Tracker who works for the FBI hunting down notorious criminals. Crossing paths with Israeli agent Dev Leitner, the two seasoned operators join forces to bring down terrorist cells, rogue assassins, and black-ops mercenaries in these adrenaline-soaked novels that span the globe.

First Wave Boxed Set

Special Forces veteran Travis Combs just wanted to forget his weary years of leading combat missions while taking an extended rafting trip through the Grand Canyon. As he and his group complete a 22-day trip on the Colorado River, they find the world has unraveled from a deadly pandemic. Now, he has to show his small band how to live off the land and cross the rugged Arizona desert, while evading blood-drinking zombies, gangs of cartel bikers, and a rogue government agency. The bestselling First Wave Series is now available as a boxed set with all three action-packed volumes. For fans of *The Walking Dead* or *World War Z*.

Until Morning Comes, Volumes 1–5

Secret Service Agent Carlie Simmons began her day surrounded by trusted colleagues in an inter-agency shooting competition in Tucson. It ended with a staggering body count as the world around her unraveled from a deadly virus. With her mission to extract the President's daughter from the University of Arizona gone awry, she must choose between her sworn duties and her moral obligations to others as the city is overtaken by roving packs of flesh-eating mutants. If she and her small group are to survive the night and find a way out of the ravaged city, she will have to summon all of her training, mental prowess, and tactical abilities.

The Emergence Series, Volumes 1-8

An epic struggle for survival between humans and a twisted mutation of undead begins in *Emergence* when a deadly virus, originating in China, quickly spreads throughout the world, turning humans into cunning predators with interconnected mental abilities. The human race is about to become an endangered species unless CIA Agent Will Reisner and his elite team can track down the source of the virus before the world is completely consumed. If you liked *The Puppet Masters, I am Legend,* or *The Strain* then check out Emergence!

ABOUT THE AUTHOR

JT Sawyer is the pen name for Tony Nester. Before becoming a fulltime writer, JT made his living teaching survival courses for the military special operations community, Department of Homeland Security, US Marshals, FAA, and other federal agencies throughout the country. He has appeared on the Travel Channel, Fox News, Discovery, in the New York Times and served as a consultant for the film *Into the Wild* along with being the author of 12 non-fiction books on bushcraft and survival.

Nowadays, JT prefers having a roof over his head and placing his fictional characters in dire situations in his thriller and post-apocalyptic books. He lives with his family in Colorado Springs, CO. Visit jtsawyer.com for more information.

Made in the USA
Monee, IL
10 May 2023

33452735R00121